'A knight's supposed to ask the woman he's in love with for her favour,' Tyler said.

Dominic and Louisa both froze.

'But I expect you'll ask Mum because I'm going to be your page and you don't want her to feel left out,' he added.

Later that evening, when Tyler had gone to bed, Dominic kissed Louisa goodbye. 'I'm sorry about earlier. For a moment I thought he'd guessed about us.'

'No. He was trying to put himself in my shoes. I think all that social skills training he's doing at school and my back-up at home is starting to pay off,' she said lightly.

'Probably.' Dominic paused. 'How do you think he'd feel? About you and me seeing each other, I mean?'

'It's still early days,' she said softly. 'Let's wait a while before we tell him.'

He nodded. 'You're right. Best to take it slowly.'

But right now his heart felt fuller and lighter than it had in years—and he knew it was thanks to her. Her warmth, her selflessness, that air of calm. Maybe, just maybe, she'd help him to forgive himself. And maybe, just maybe, he could do something for her, too. Repair some of the damage that Jack had inflicted when he'd rejected her and their son.

Kate Hardy lives in Norwich, in the east of England, with her husband, two young children, one bouncy spaniel, and too many books to count! When she's not busy writing romance or researching local history, she helps out at her children's schools. She also loves cooking—spot the recipes sneaked into her books! (They're also on her website, along with extracts and stories behind the books.) Writing for Mills & Boon has been a dream come true for Kate—something she wanted to do ever since she was twelve. She's been writing Medical^{TM} Romances for nearly five years now, and also writes for Modern Heat^{TM}. She says it's the best of both worlds, because she gets to learn lots of new things when she's researching the background to a book: add a touch of passion, drama and danger, a new gorgeous hero every time, and it's the perfect job!

Kate's always delighted to hear from readers, so do drop in to her website at www.katehardy.com

Recent titles by the same author:

Medical^{TM} Romance
NEUROSURGEON...AND MUM!
THE DOCTOR'S LOST-AND-FOUND BRIDE
FALLING FOR THE PLAYBOY MILLIONAIRE
  The Brides of Penhally Bay

Modern Heat^{TM}
RED WINE AND HER SEXY EX*
CHAMPAGNE WITH A CELEBRITY*
GOOD GIRL OR GOLD-DIGGER?

Château Lefèvre linked duo

A CHRISTMAS KNIGHT

BY
KATE HARDY

First published in Great Britain 2010
by Mills & Boon,
an imprint of Harlequin (UK) Limited,
Large Print edition 2011
Eton House, 18-24 Paradise Road,
Richmond, Surrey TW9 1SR

© Pamela Brooks 2010

ISBN: 978 0 263 21742 1

AudioGo 14 JUN 2011

Printed and bound in Great Britain
by CPI Antony Rowe, Chippenham, Wiltshire

For Benita Brown
With many thanks for the story
about her wonderful GP father
and the milkman's horse

CHAPTER ONE

'LET me get you a coffee, and then I'll take you round and introduce you to the team,' Essie, the charge nurse, said with a smile.

'Thanks. I, um, brought some biscuits for the staffroom,' Louisa said, handing her a large tin.

'Thanks very much.' Essie beamed as she peered at the lid. 'Chocolate ones, too. Excellent. You'll fit right in.' She gave Louisa a sympathetic look. 'The first day's always the worst, isn't it? Like being back at school.'

Louisa smiled back. 'I've been doing agency work for the last three months, so you'd think I'd be used to change. But, yes, you're right. It feels like the first day at school, when you don't know anyone and you don't know the routine—well, as much of a routine as you get in the emergency department,' she finished. No two days were ever quite the same.

'You'll be fine,' Essie told her warmly. 'I've

rostered you onto Minors—but if anything big comes in, I might need to borrow you for Resus.'

'That's fine,' Louisa said. As a nurse practitioner, she was able to see patients through from start to finish for the less serious problems—from taking the medical history through to doing the clinical examination, ordering and interpreting tests, diagnosing the ailment and organising a treatment plan for the patient. She loved the responsibility and the feeling that she was in charge of her own day, but she also enjoyed the busy, hands-on role in Resus, working as part of a team.

'Dominic's the senior registrar in Resus today. He's our resident heart-throb,' Essie said with a grin. 'He looks like Prince Charming.'

Heart-throb. Jack had been a heart-throb, too. But he'd been very far from being Prince Charming. He'd walked out on Louisa just when she'd needed him most. So much for promising to love, honour and cherish her. Jack had left her—and Tyler—because he couldn't handle the idea of having a son with Asperger's. As soon as Jack had heard the paediatrician say the words 'autistic spectrum disorder', he'd closed off, and Louisa had seen it in his eyes. She'd known that her marriage was cracking beyond repair, and there was nothing she could do to stop it. Less than two months later, he'd moved out and asked her for a divorce.

She could cope with Jack's rejection of her; but she'd never, ever forgive him for rejecting their bright, quirky, gorgeous son. And she'd taken notice of the old saying, ever since: *Handsome is as handsome does.*

Essie didn't seem to notice Louisa's silence. 'He's been here for eight years now. He joined us as a wet-behind-the-ears house officer, and worked his way up.' She sighed. 'Though he's not one for settling down, our Dominic. Women used to fall at his feet in droves, but nowadays he doesn't even date—he's completely wrapped up in his work. Pity, because he'd make a fantastic husband and father.'

Louisa had already spotted the photograph on Essie's desk; the charge nurse was smiling for the camera, looking blissfully happy with her husband and two children. It seemed that Essie was the type who wanted everyone to be as happy and settled as she was. Well, she *was* happy and settled. She just wasn't in a two-parent family. 'Marriage isn't for everyone,' she said quietly.

'You're not married, then?'

'Not any more.' Not that she wanted to talk about it. Though, given the photograph on Essie's desk, she could offer the perfect distraction. 'But I do have a gorgeous son. Tyler.' She took a photograph from her purse to show the charge nurse.

'Oh, he looks a sweetie. And he's so like you.'

'He is,' she agreed with a smile. 'I'm really lucky.' And she meant it. Tyler was the light of her life, and she loved him with a fierceness that she knew probably made her protect him too much.

'So how old is he?' Essie asked.

'Eight. He started middle school last week— so this summer was the least disruptive time to move here from London.' Louisa took a deep breath. 'Actually, that's why I started today, not last week—I wanted to give him a few days to settle in to his new school first.'

'It's always hard, changing schools, whether you're from the local first school or not,' Essie agreed. 'Though I'm sure he'll soon make friends.'

Louisa would be very, very surprised if he did. Tyler was self-contained in the extreme. Having Asperger's meant he saw the world in terms of black and white, with no shades of grey. Other children quickly noticed that—especially as Ty was a walking encyclopaedia on his favourite subjects, and wouldn't hesitate to correct anyone instead of just letting it go for the sake of social harmony. She'd tried to help him, inviting children home for tea after school—but Tyler had never been invited back. Probably because most of the time, when someone came over, he'd lose interest in whatever game they were playing, disappear up to his room and start drawing. 'Maybe,' she said.

'Give it a week and he'll be playing football with the rest of them,' Essie said cheerfully.

Louisa wrinkled her nose. 'He's not really into football.'

'Computer games, then?' Essie asked. 'Tell me about it. My eldest is glued to his console.'

'What Ty really likes is horses. I'm going to ring round the local riding stables to see if there are any places for lessons.' Louisa had read an article about how good riding could be for children with Asperger's; it was just a matter of finding the right stables, one that could accommodate Tyler without making a big deal out of things. And maybe he'd find it easier to make friends with children who shared his passion.

'Horses?' Essie looked thoughtful. 'Then you definitely need to talk to Dominic. He's got a horse. He's bound to know a good riding school locally.'

Louisa smiled politely, but she had no intention of asking a heart-throb for help. She'd already learned the hard way that heart-throbs weren't reliable—and she'd never, ever take any risks with her son.

Essie had introduced Louisa to everyone except the resus team when her bleep went off.

'Resus—and I'm needed,' she said ruefully, glancing at the display. 'Sorry. Can I leave you with Jess to open up Minors?'

'Sure. No worries,' Louisa said.

Her first case was a seven-year-old girl who'd fallen and bent her fingers back the previous day; now her hand was stiff and swollen.

'I know I should've brought her here earlier. I thought she'd just banged herself and was making a fuss, and it'd settle down,' Mrs Aldiss said, chewing her bottom lip.

'That's often the case, after a fall,' Louisa reassured her. 'It's a tough one to call. Have you given her anything for the pain?'

'I've been giving her paracetamol, and I put an ice pack on her hand yesterday.'

'That's good.' She crouched down so she was on a level with the little girl. 'Hello, I'm Louisa—and you're being ever so brave, Pippa,' she said with a smile. 'Can I have a look at your hand, so I can see what's wrong and make it better?'

The little girl was white-faced, but she nodded.

Gently, Louisa examined her fingers. 'Can you make a fist for me?' she asked, showing Pippa exactly what she wanted her to do.

The little girl tried, but her sharp intake of breath told Louisa that it was just too painful.

'OK, sweetheart, you can stop trying now. You've done really well,' Louisa reassured her. 'I don't want to do anything that'll make it hurt more. But what I do want to do is see what's making it hurt so much, so I'm going to send you to X-Ray. It's not going to hurt, but they have special cameras there to take a picture of your bones so I can see if you've broken your finger or whether you've hurt one of the ligaments—that's the bit that helps you bend your finger.' She ruffled the little girl's hair. 'And once I know that, I'll know how to treat you. If it's just a little break, I'll do what we call buddy taping—that means I'll strap your poorly finger to the one next door, to help it mend.'

'If it's a big break, will she need a plaster on her hand?' Mrs Aldiss asked.

'It depends on the break. But I'd definitely recommend resting her hand in a sling. If you can just wait here for a second, I'll make sure Pippa's booked in with X-Ray and they know exactly what I want to see,' Louisa said.

Mrs Aldiss cuddled the little girl. 'And we'll have a story while we're waiting, OK, honey?'

Louisa swiftly booked a slot in X-Ray, explained what she was looking for, and then went back to her patient. Pippa's mother was clearly near the end of the story, so Louisa waited for her to finish. 'You're very good at that.'

'It's Pip's favourite. I've read it that many times, I know it off by heart,' Mrs Aldiss said.

Louisa smiled at them and took a sticker out of her pocket. 'I'll see you again after you've gone to X-Ray, Pippa, but in the meantime I think you deserve one of my special stickers for being really brave.'

'Thank you,' Pippa said shyly, brightening slightly at the sight of the glittery badge.

Louisa directed Mrs Aldiss to the X-ray department, then went to collect the notes for her next patient.

The morning was busy, with a steady stream of patients; when Pippa came back after her X-ray and Louisa pulled the file up on the computer screen, she was relieved to see it was a stable fracture.

'See this little tiny mark on here?' she asked. 'That's where you've broken your finger. So what I'm going to do is strap it to the finger next to it, to be a buddy to keep the poorly one straight.' Gently, she strapped up the little girl's finger. 'You need to rest your hand, sweetheart, so I'm going to give you a sling—that will help you keep your hand up and make the swelling go down, so it doesn't hurt so much. And I'd like you to come back in a week's time for another X-ray so we can see how well it's healing.'

'How long will she need her fingers like that?' Mrs Aldiss asked.

'Usually it's three or four weeks, and then another couple of weeks where you keep the hand rested—not too much exercise, and I'm afraid that includes using games consoles.'

'Just as well it's you and not your brother, then,' Mrs Aldiss said ruefully, 'or we'd really be in trouble!'

'It is your writing hand, Pippa?' Louisa asked.

Pippa shook her head. 'So I can still draw?'

'You can definitely still draw.' Louisa smiled at her.

'I'll bring you a picture when I come back,' Pippa said.

'I'd love that. I've only just moved to this department,' Louisa said, 'so I have a whole wall that's just waiting for pictures. I'll see you in a week, sweetheart. Remember to rest your hand as much as you can.'

Things had quietened down slightly, just after lunchtime, when Essie came into the office where

Louisa was catching up with paperwork. 'The lull before the storm, hmm?' she asked.

'Probably. So I'm making the most of it and sorting out this lot,' Louisa said, gesturing to the notes and the pile of letters she was working through.

'Can I borrow you for a minute to meet the resus team? They're on a break—and very grateful for your biscuits, I might add.'

Essie continued chatting until they reached the rest room, and then introduced her to the resus team. 'This is Sally, our student nurse.'

Sally greeted her warmly, and then Essie motioned to the man who was sitting apart from the others, reading a medical journal.

'Louisa, this is Dominic Hurst, our senior reg. Dominic—Louisa Austin, our new nurse practitioner.'

Essie had described him as looking like Prince Charming. And that wasn't the half of it, Louisa thought. Dominic Hurst looked like a Pre-Raphaelite painting of a medieval prince, all dark flowing locks and fair skin and chiselled cheekbones and dark, dark eyes. Even dressed simply in a plain white shirt, sober tie and dark trousers, he was incredibly striking. No wonder women fell at his feet in droves. He was tall—just over six feet, she'd guess—and, at close range, those navy-blue eyes were devastating. Not to mention that beautiful mouth, which sent all kinds of crazy thoughts spinning through her head.

'Pleased to meet you, Dr Hurst,' she said politely.

He looked up from the journal and blinked. 'Sorry?'

'Dominic, I can't believe you're still working when you're on a break.' Essie rolled her eyes. 'You didn't hear a word I just said, did you?'

''Fraid not. I was reading.' He gave her a wry smile. 'Sorry.'

'This is Louisa Austin, our new nurse practitioner,' Essie repeated.

'Pleased to meet you, Nurse Practitioner Austin.'

Dominic's handshake was firm, precise and brief—and it felt as if an electric current was running through her veins. Which was crazy, because she never reacted like that to anyone. It hadn't even been like that with Jack, in the good days. So why now? And why this man?

'Louisa's looking for riding lessons, because her son likes horses,' Essie continued, and Dominic's expression turned wary.

Oh, for pity's sake, did he think she was going to use her child as an excuse to come on to him? Still, she wasn't going to be rude to him. 'He does indeed. He wants to be a knight when he grows up,' Louisa said, keeping her tone light.

If anything, Dominic's expression grew even warier. She didn't have the faintest idea why, but despite Essie's suggestion she wasn't going to bother asking him if he could recommend any riding stables locally. Clearly he'd take it the wrong way, so she'd be better off doing what she always did and sorting it out for herself.

Dominic Hurst might look like Prince Charming, but he definitely didn't have a charming manner. She sincerely hoped he was better in a work situation, for the sake of his patients and his colleagues. She made a polite murmur, and to her relief Essie stepped in again. 'Let me introduce you to Sasha and Ronnie,' Essie said, and swept Louisa over to where two women were making coffee.

* * *

Dominic took a gulp of coffee. Whatever was the matter with him? It was the poor woman's first day in the department and he'd been rude to her.

Well, not rude, *exactly*—he had at least acknowledged her and shaken her hand.

But the zing of attraction when her skin had touched his had thrown him, made him tongue-tied. Which was crazy, because he was never that boorish. Essie had even given him an opening, saying that Louisa was looking for riding lessons for her child. He could've given her Ric and Bea's number, because he knew they had a couple of spaces on their list. They'd talked about it last night, how people were cutting back on extras in the recession and riding lessons were expensive, and Bea had suggested that they should hold an open day to get people interested in the stables.

But then Louisa had said something that slammed right through him. *He wants to be a knight when he grows up.* Yeah. Been there, done that, and the absolute worst had happened.

Though that wasn't her fault and he shouldn't have taken it out on her.

He'd apologise later, and hopefully she wouldn't

hold it against him if she was needed to work with his team in Resus.

Riding lessons. For her son.

Though she wasn't wearing a wedding ring. And there wasn't a tell-tale band of pale skin on her finger to say she'd removed it for work. He'd looked. And he was cross with himself for looking.

Dominic took another gulp of coffee, needing the bitter liquid to jolt some sense back into him. Louisa Austin was gorgeous, with beautiful grey eyes and long dark hair; she'd tied it back hygienically for work, but he could imagine what it looked like loose. Like waves of shiny silk. Her mouth was a perfect rosebud, and it sent a shiver of pure desire running through him, along with an insane urge to find out how it would feel against his own mouth. It had been a long, long time since he'd felt an attraction that strong and that immediate—and that was what had thrown him most.

He knew that it would be pretty stupid to act on that attraction. He wasn't in the market for a relationship; and, even if he was, Louisa had a son. Which meant that either she was already spoken for, despite the lack of a wedding ring, or she was a single parent who'd be wary of taking any risks in a relationship, for her child's sake, and would want someone responsible in her life.

Responsible.

Right.

Which was about as far from him as you could get: hadn't he ruined his brother's life, two years ago?

He needed to get out of here. Now.

'No rest for the wicked,' he said, striding over to the sink and rinsing out his mug. 'If we're to have any chance of meeting our targets today, I'd better get back out there and hope Resus stays quiet for the rest of the afternoon. Welcome to the team, Nurse Practitioner Austin.' And he left the rest room before he could do anything ridiculous. Like asking her to have lunch with him tomorrow so they could get to know each other a little better.

The rest of Louisa's shift turned out to be as busy as the morning, but she managed to get to the after-school club on time to meet Tyler.

'Hi, Mum.' He gave her the shy smile that always made her melt.

'How was your day, honey?' She gave him a hug.

'OK.'

'Best bit?'

'Lunch. We had pasta. It wasn't as good as yours, though.'

She really hoped that he hadn't actually said that to the dinner ladies. She could still remember the time they'd had Sunday lunch at her best friend's house and then, when asked if he'd enjoyed it, he'd very politely thanked Mel and gone on to tell her that her gravy was slimy and her potatoes weren't nice and crispy on the outside and fluffy in the middle like his mother's were. Luckily Mel hadn't taken it to heart, but Louisa had had to explain to Tyler that sometimes it was OK to tell a little fib so you didn't hurt people's feelings. And even after she'd finished explaining, he still didn't get it. 'Let's go home and make dinner. Do you have any spellings or times tables I need to test you on?'

'No. Do you want to see the horse I drew at

lunchtime?' He had his sketchbook out of his schoolbag as soon as he'd put his seat belt on.

She stared at the drawing in awe. 'It's beautiful, darling.' The horse was drawn in painstaking detail, and was incredibly realistic. Tyler really did have a talent for art—something she could only assume came from Jack's side, because nobody in her side of the family was arty. But there was nobody to ask, because Jack's family had severed all connection with them as soon as Jack had left—and for the same reason.

Though it didn't bother her any more. She knew that she and Ty were better off without them. Her parents accepted Tyler as he was and gave him enough love for two sets of grandparents. They didn't need the Listons.

Tyler disappeared to his room as soon as they got home, and Louisa knew exactly what he was doing. Putting his drawing in a plastic wallet, labelling it and adding it to his database. One good thing about having a son who was obsessed with order was that she never had to tell him to tidy his bedroom. It was always immaculate. Smiling, she busied herself preparing dinner, and when everything was ready she called him down, careful not to let the new potatoes, chicken or vegetables touch each other on Tyler's plate.

He chattered happily about horses all the way through dinner; and then it was the usual routine of washing up while he had a bath, nagging him to clean his teeth, and giving him a kiss goodnight.

Carefully, he turned the kitchen timer next to his bed to twenty minutes. 'I'll put my light out as soon as the alarm goes off, Mum,' he promised.

And she knew he would, even if he was in midsentence. Tyler was one for sticking to the rules. 'See you in the morning, darling. Sleep well,' she said, giving him another kiss.

Then she curled up on the sofa with her laptop and looked up all the local riding stables, listing them with their phone numbers in her diary. She'd start calling them tomorrow. It was a pity that Dominic Hurst had turned out to be so formal and unapproachable—she would've appreciated some tips on choosing the right riding school. But she was used to doing things on her own, so she wasn't going to let it throw her.

And as for stray thoughts of a tall, dark, gorgeous and reserved medic with a mouth that promised sin…she'd banish them all from her head, because there just wasn't room in her life for someone like that.

Handsome is as handsome does.

CHAPTER TWO

TUESDAY went without incident in Minors, but on Wednesday Louisa was called in to help in Resus.

'Essie tells me you're very experienced, so I'd like you to work with me, please, Nurse Practitioner Austin,' Dominic said.

She noticed again that he'd addressed her by her title rather than by her name. Was he just being like that with her because she was new, or was he like that with everyone? Then she remembered that Essie had called him by his first name. Better get things straight now, then. 'OK, but can we spend thirty seconds now to save us a lot of time when our patients arrive?' she asked.

He frowned. 'How do you mean?'

'It goes without saying that I respect your seniority, but I'm used to working on first-name terms. It's quicker, easier, and less of a mouthful. Would you mind?'

He blinked. 'OK, Nu—Louisa.'

'Thank you, Dominic.' She used his name deliberately. 'So what's happened?'

'Car crash. Three casualties,' Dominic explained. 'Both drivers are coming in with suspected whiplash, and the passenger has suspected multiple fractures. Ronnie and Sasha are going to treat the drivers, and I need you with me as lead nurse to treat the passenger—Sally will assist us.'

She nodded. 'How long have we got to prepare?'

'Five minutes. I'm going down to the ambulance bay now.'

She busied herself getting the trolley ready; when Dominic came back with the paramedic and their patient, the team swung into action.

'Rhiannon, this is my team, Louisa and Sally,' Dominic said calmly. 'They're going to help me look after you.'

'Hurts,' Rhiannon mumbled. 'Where's Gary?'

'Your husband's right here,' he reassured her. 'Ronnie's looking after him, and as soon as she's checked him over and made him comfortable, he'll be able to come and see you. And we're going to give something to help with the pain,' he said. 'I'm going to put an oxygen mask on you to help you breathe better, and then we're going to have a proper look at you, OK?'

On Dominic's direction, Sally gently cut through Rhiannon's clothes so he could do a full body assessment, top to toe. Meanwhile, Louisa hooked Rhiannon up to a cardiac monitor, put in a second line and started taking obs.

'Heart rate 135, respirations twenty-six, blood pressure 82/54,' she said. Tachycardia and low blood pressure pointed to major loss of blood—probably caused by internal injuries, Louisa thought.

'We need to get some fluids in. Start with a litre of Hartmann's, and get six units cross-matched for me,' Dominic said—and looked approving when he saw that she already had the saline solution in her hand.

Dominic had given Rhiannon painkillers to make her more comfortable; but when her blood pressure didn't respond to the fluids and her sats started dropping, he glanced at Louisa. 'Can you do ABGs for me, please, Louisa? And, Sally, I need X-rays.' He listened to Rhiannon's chest.

From the bruising on Rhiannon's skin, it looked

as if she had several broken ribs. No doubt
Dominic wanted to check for pulmonary contusions. There were a lot of problems that could be
caused by blunt trauma at high velocity, Louisa
knew; with damage in Rhiannon's chest area,
there could be trauma to the heart as well as the
lungs.

'I think we need to intubate.' He held Rhiannon's
hand as he explained to her what they were doing.
'You're struggling to breathe, sweetheart, so we
need to help you with that and make sure you
get enough oxygen. I'm going to put a tube down
your throat so you won't be able to speak, but I'm
going to give you some medication first so you
won't feel it and it won't hurt—it'll make you
more comfortable. I know you're feeling tired and
it's hard to talk, so just squeeze my hand if you're
OK with that—once for yes and twice for no.' He
paused. 'That's a yes—that's my girl. We'll get
you comfortable as soon as we can.'

Louisa was just drawing up the ampoules of
anaesthetic when one of the drivers who'd been
brought in came over to them, his face ashen.
'Oh, my God, Rhi! I'm so sorry. I couldn't avoid
him—he just pulled out on me and there was

nothing I could do.' He looked distraught as he stared wildly at Dominic and Louisa. 'I can't believe I've come out with just bruises, and Rhi's so…so…' His voice caught.

'Gary, isn't it?' Dominic said, somehow managing to divide his attention and eye contact between his patient and her husband.

'Yes.'

'She was asking for you.'

'Can I hold her hand?' At Dominic's brief nod, Gary curled his fingers round his wife. 'Honey, I'm here, and I love you, and I'm so sorry.' He dragged in a breath and looked pleadingly at Dominic. 'Is she going to die?'

'Not on my shift,' Dominic said, 'though it might be easier on you if you wait outside. There's a vending machine just round the corner. I promise we'll come and find you as soon as we've got her stable and let you know what's going on, but for now we need to concentrate on Rhiannon here and treat her.'

Gary shook his head. 'No. I need to stay with her.'

'Unless you're a trained medic, it can look very worrying in here,' Dominic said gently.

'Especially as we're just about to intubate her to help her breathe. Trust me, we're going to do everything we can for your wife, but it will be much better on your nerves if you go and get yourself a hot drink and leave us to it for the next few minutes.'

'I'll come and get you as soon as there's any news,' Louisa promised. But she noticed that Gary was staring at his wife, looking stunned. In shock, she thought—not the medical kind, but the emotional kind. They needed to get him out of here. 'Do I have two minutes, Dominic, to show Gary where everything is?'

'Two minutes,' Dominic confirmed; the expression in his eyes told Louisa that he knew exactly what she was doing and approved. Which was a huge relief: he was much easier to work with than she'd expected. And he was sensitive with patients and relatives. Maybe she'd just caught him on a bad day on Monday.

'Come on, I'll show you where the drinks machine is,' Louisa said, slipping her arm through Gary's and guiding him out of Resus.

'I was coming down the hill. I wasn't speeding. I could see the other car approaching the junction, but he wasn't even indicating! And then he just pulled out in front of me. It was as if it all happened in slow motion. I could see we were going to crash, and I couldn't do anything to stop it. I slammed on the brakes, but it wasn't enough.' Gary shivered. 'We hit him and the car spun round. Rhi's side of the car was squashed against another one. And...' He covered his face with his hands. 'She *can't* die. We celebrated our twenty-fifth wedding anniversary last week. I can't... Not without her...'

Louisa got him a cup of hot, sweet tea from the vending machine—even if he didn't normally take sugar or drink tea, she knew it would help— and settled him in a chair. 'Gary, it wasn't your fault, and the staff here are really good,' she told him gently. 'We're going to do our very, very best. Now I have to go back and help Dominic treat Rhiannon, but I'll be back as soon as I can with any news.' She squeezed his shoulder. 'I know waiting's hard but hang on in there, love.'

'You're so kind. Thank you. And please—' Gary's face was stricken '—please, don't let my wife die.'

By the time Louisa got back into Resus, the

medication had taken effect, and Dominic started to intubate their patient. She'd seen it done before, but never with this calm, confident efficiency—and he was amazingly quick.

Dominic Hurst was a superb doctor, she thought. And she liked the way he'd made time to talk to his patient and her husband, clearly aware of how important communication was as a way of bringing down stress levels.

He blew up the cuff on the tube and turned to the other nurse. 'Sally, are they ready for us in Radiology?'

'Yes.'

'Great. Thanks for that. Can you bleep the orthopods, please, and let them know we have a patient with suspected flail chest? I want to have a look at the X-rays, so I'm going down to Radiology with Rhiannon.'

'Do you want me to give ITU a call, to put them on standby?' Louisa asked quietly, so Rhiannon couldn't hear her and start to worry. In her experience, it was best to involve the intensive care unit as early as possible, because cases of pulmonary contusions often led to ARDS—adult respiratory distress syndrome. And if there were multiple broken ribs, she'd need careful monitoring.

'Yes, please. And could you tell Gary I'm taking her to X-Ray? Not because he should worry himself sick, but because it means I can see the X-rays straight off and it'll save us some time. Tell him I'll come and talk to him as soon as we know more.' He smiled at her. 'Thank you, Sally. You've done a really good job. You, too, Louisa. Even though this is the first time we've worked together, it's felt as if we've been on the same team for years. Your old department must really be missing you.'

The compliment made her feel warm all over—especially as she hadn't expected it from him. And it was good to work with a doctor who appreciated the nursing staff rather than taking them for granted, especially one who bothered to give a student praise where it was due. She smiled back at him. 'Thanks.'

While Dominic went off to X-Ray with Rhiannon, Louisa contacted the intensive care unit to put them in the picture, then went in search of Gary to let him know what was happening.

'Is she going to be all right?' he asked. 'I'll

never forgive myself if anything happens to her. And that stupid guy who tried to get into a gap that wasn't there, just to save a few seconds...' He was shaking, clearly near tears.

Louisa put her arm round him. 'I know, love. You said yourself there was nothing you could do, so don't blame yourself. The police will deal with the other driver.' Who'd also walked away without a scratch, according to Ronnie, but that wasn't something Louisa intended to share. 'We'll know a lot more when the X-rays are back, and Dominic will talk you through what Rhiannon's injuries are and how we're going to treat her. But for now we're keeping her comfortable. Try not to worry—and, yes, I know that's a lot easier said than done.' She gave him a sympathetic smile. 'Is there anyone we can call for you?'

'I... No.' He shook his head. 'I'd better call our daughter myself. She'll be devastated.' He dragged in a breath. 'I can't use a mobile phone here, can I?'

'In the corridors, you can,' she reassured him. 'The phone won't interfere with equipment there.' It wasn't the only reason the hospital preferred not to have people chatting on mobile phones—loud conversations disturbed other patients, and some ringtones sounded eerily like alarms on equipment. The blanket ban on mobile phones throughout the hospital had been relaxed, except for critical-care areas such as the emergency department, the coronary care unit and the special care baby unit, where equipment could be affected by electromagnetic interference.

'Thank you.'

When Dominic came back from Resus, he looked serious but calm. 'Gary, I've seen the scans and I'm sending Rhiannon up to Theatre where the surgeons can help her. She's got four ribs broken in two places, pulmonary contusions— that's a bruise on the lung and you often get that with broken ribs—and what looks to me like a cut to her liver.'

'So the surgeons can fix her ribs?'

'They might decide to let them heal without fixing them,' Dominic said. 'But the contusions are going to make it a bit hard for Rhiannon to breathe, so she'll be in Intensive Care afterwards until they heal—they can keep a close eye on her and make sure she's comfortable.'

'You mean she's going to be ventilated?' Gary's eyes widened. 'Oh, my God.'

'It looks and sounds a lot scarier than it is. It's going to be the best treatment for her,' Dominic reassured him. 'We're taking her up to Theatre now, and if you'd like to you can come with us, as far as the doors. There's a waiting area there, and one of the surgeons will come out and talk you through what's happening. The staff at the ICU—the intensive care unit—are lovely, and they'll be happy to answer any questions you have.'

They headed up to Theatre, Gary holding his wife's hand all the way.

'I'm so sorry, Rhi. I love you,' he said, clearly trying to hold back tears.

'They'll take care of her,' Louisa said gently, putting her arm round his shoulders as Rhiannon was wheeled through the doors to Theatre. 'Is your daughter coming?'

'She's on her way.' He bit his lip. 'And I'm keeping you from your work.'

'That's OK.' If necessary, she'd work through her lunch hour to make sure that the targets were hit. People came before admin, in her book, and always would; and if she had to explain herself to the bean-counters, so be it. Nursing was about people, not numbers. 'I'll wait until she gets here.'

When Gary and Rhiannon's daughter arrived, Louisa explained what had happened and what would happen next, made sure they both had a hot drink, then headed back down to the emergency department. She was back in Minors as nurse practitioner for the rest of her shift, and her lunch break consisted of two minutes to bolt a sandwich so that she could catch up with the delay in treating her patients. When it was clear that she was still running late, she made a quick call to her mother to ask if she could pick up Ty from after-school club, and continued working steadily through her list. After she'd seen her last patient, she headed for Resus, hoping that Dominic would be there and that he knew how Rhiannon was.

'Shouldn't you have been off duty half an hour ago?' he asked.

She shrugged. 'It happens. I just wondered if you'd heard anything from the ICU about Rhiannon?'

'Yes, I have.' He smiled at her.

Without that reserve, he was truly stunning; her heart felt as if it had just done a somersault. Which was crazy, because she wasn't looking to feel this way about anyone. She didn't need a relationship to complicate her life.

'Do you have time for a quick coffee while I fill you in?' he asked. 'I could do with a Danish pastry.'

That sounded dangerously close to a date. Even though Essie had said he was wrapped up in his work rather than relationships, she didn't want Dominic to get the wrong idea. Especially as she was aware of how attractive she found him. 'Sorry, I can't. I need to pick up my son. Mum met him for me, but he hates it when I'm late.'

'Can I give you a lift home and tell you on the way?' he asked.

'Thanks for the offer, but my car's in the staff car park.'

'Then how about I walk you to your car while I tell you about Rhiannon?'

She nodded. 'That'd be good. Thanks. I'll just get my bag from my locker.' She hurried off to collect her things. 'So what did they say?' she asked when she returned and Dominic walked with her to the car park.

'Rhiannon's pulled through—the surgeons fixed the liver damage and stopped the bleeding. She's got an epidural in for pain relief, and she's going to be observed in ICU for a while to make sure she doesn't develop pneumonia.'

'Did they wire her ribs?'

'They decided against surgical correction of her flail chest, because the ventilator will make sure her lungs are working properly and aren't compromised by her ribs,' he said. 'As soon as the contusions are resolved, provided there aren't any secondary complications, she can come off ventilation. I popped in to see how she was doing and have a chat with Gary. They've warned him that her breathing is going to get slightly worse before it gets better—on the same principle that a bruise always hurts more the day after—but now he knows she's got a good chance, he's relaxed a bit.'

'His daughter's nice,' Louisa said. 'She'll support them both through it.'

He looked at her and raised an eyebrow. 'You didn't have a lunch break either, did you?'

'Yes, I did,' she protested.

He gave her a wry smile. 'Long enough to scoff a chocolate bar, hmm?'

'A chicken wrap, actually. I don't like chocolate.'

He looked surprised. 'You must be the first medic I've ever met who doesn't think it's a food group. And didn't you bring in a tin of chocolate biscuits the other day?'

'Yes—because most people like them.'

'So you're more of a savoury person?' he asked.

'I love cheese scones,' she said. 'And hot buttered toast with Marmite.'

'That's utterly revolting,' he said, pulling a face. 'So where did you work before here?'

'The London Victoria. It's where I did my training.'

'It's got a good reputation. What made you come to the George IV?' he asked.

'The nurse practitioner post was vacant—plus my parents wanted to retire to the coast. I know London's only an hour and a half from Brighton, but Ty adores his grandparents and I wanted to be able to stay close to them.'

'So your husband was able to move his job, too, or is he commuting to London?'

'Ex.' She took a deep breath. 'And Ty's father isn't part of our lives. At all.'

He grimaced. 'Sorry. That was nosey of me, and I didn't mean to stomp on a sore spot.'

She shrugged. 'It's OK. I guess the only way you get to know a new colleague is to ask questions.'

'True.' Dominic looked wary. 'And I owe you an apology from the other day. I'm not normally that rude.'

'I didn't think anything of it.'

'Yes, you did—otherwise you wouldn't have been so sharp with me in Resus this morning.'

She bit her lip. She had been a bit sharp with him. 'I'm sorry I was—well, snotty with you.'

'I understand why. Anyway, there isn't room for egos in our business. The patients should always come first.'

Her sentiments exactly. 'I think we started off on the wrong foot.'

'Agreed, and I'm sorry, too. For the sake of a decent working relationship, can we start again?'

She was all in favour of decent working relationships. 'Louisa Austin, nurse practitioner. Pleased to meet you.' She stretched out her hand.

He shook it; again, it felt as if electricity bubbled through her veins, but she ignored the sensation. This was *work*.

'Dominic Hurst, senior ED reg. Pleased to meet you, too, Louisa.' He paused. 'You said you were looking for riding lessons for your son. I assume Essie told you I have a horse? My best friend owns the stables where I keep him. I could have a word with him and his wife.'

'Thanks, but there's no point. He won't have a space.'

He frowned. 'How do you mean?'

'I've already tried ringing round some of the local riding schools and…well, their lists are all full.'

He looked surprised. 'We're in a recession and riding lessons are one of the first things that tend to get cut, because they're not cheap—instead of going twice a week, people go riding maybe once a fortnight instead.'

Just as she'd thought. Especially when the waiting lists had suddenly become two years long.

Might as well get it over with now. 'The thing is, my son has Asperger's.'

He shrugged. 'And?'

'The riding schools I rang changed their minds about having places when I explained.'

'More fool them. Riding's really good for Asperger's kids. Being with horses helps them learn to understand non-verbal body language.'

Now that she really hadn't expected. She was more used to people being uncomfortable around Ty. Understanding like this was rare. 'Did you used to work in paediatrics, or do you know someone with Asperger's?'

'I know someone,' he said, 'and horses have made a huge difference to him. But I can remember his parents used to worry themselves sick about him, because he never seemed to make friends at school. I guess you probably do the same with your son.'

'All the time,' she admitted, caught off guard.

'Don't,' he said softly. 'He'll be fine. He might only have one or two really close friends, but they'll be good ones—and that's better than having hundreds of acquaintances you can't really rely on when life gets tough. And if he finds a job that matches the things he's interested in and doesn't involve having to deal with people whose minds aren't quite as quick as his, he'll shine.'

She blinked back the sudden rush of tears. How ridiculous. Just because someone understood, instead of making unfair judgements.

'Look, I'm going straight to the stables from here. I'll talk to Ric and Bea tonight, and then maybe you can come and have a look round at the weekend, meet the team, and see if Tyler likes the place.'

'That's very kind of you. Are you sure?'

'They do a lot of work with the RDA—Riding for the Disabled Association,' Dominic said.

Louisa's chin came up. 'Tyler isn't disabled. He just happens to have a diagnosis of Asperger's Syndrome.'

Dominic sucked in a breath. 'Sorry, I didn't mean it to sound like that. What I mean is, Ric and Bea believe in inclusion and it doesn't matter who you are or what your particular challenges are—if you love horses and want to ride, then you should have the chance to do it. Ric's parents owned the riding school before they retired and Ric took over, and they were the ones who started the RDA work at the stables. So Tyler won't be made to feel that he's a special case or anything—he'll be treated just like everyone else.'

Again, the tears threatened. How long had it been since people outside her own family and her best friend had treated her precious son just like anybody else? 'Thank you.'

'You're welcome.'

'He's eight,' she warned, 'and he's only ever ridden a horse at one of the farm park type places. He's a complete novice.'

'Bea's a brilliant teacher. She's great with kids and she's really patient with novices. I'll talk it over with her tonight. See you tomorrow,' he said as they reached her car.

'See you tomorrow. And, Dominic?' She gave him a heartfelt smile. 'Thank you.'

CHAPTER THREE

'WHAT happened?' Louisa asked.

Mrs Livesey was ashen with worry, cradling her two-year-old son. 'It's all my fault. The children were playing nicely and I was chatting to my friend over coffee—I should've been watching them more closely. Julian slipped and cut his head open on the piano. I put a cold wet cloth on it to try and stop the bleeding, but it wouldn't stop, so I brought him here.'

'That was the best thing to do,' Louisa reassured her. 'Scalp wounds always bleed a lot, so they often look worse than they are. Has Julian been sick at all, or had any kind of fit?'

'No.'

'Did he black out, or has he been drowsy since?'

Mrs Livesey shook her head.

'That's good,' Louisa said. She assessed the little boy's limb movements, then shone a light into his eyes; she was relieved to see that his pupils were equal and reactive. She took his pulse and temperature—both of which were in the normal range—and gently examined the cut on his head. 'It's clean—you did brilliantly there,' she told Mrs Livesey, 'but it's a little bit too deep just to glue it.'

'Glue it?'

'You'd be amazed at what we can do nowadays,' Louisa said with a smile. 'I'm going to put a couple of stitches in there, because it will heal better with less scarring.' She stroked Julian's hair. 'I'm going to put some magic cream on your head now to stop it hurting. But to make the magic work even better, we're going to have to sing a song. Do you know "Twinkle Twinkle Little Star"?'

'Yes,' the little boy said. 'Tinkle tinkle.'

'And can you waggle your fingers like starlight?' She demonstrated, and he copied her.

'Brilliant,' she said. 'And we'll get Mummy to sing, too, shall we?' From experience, Louisa knew that often parents needed as much distraction as toddlers. And Julian was giving a normal two-year-old's verbal response, which made

Louisa fairly sure that the worst of his injuries was the cut.

Once the cream had numbed his skin, she got Mrs Livesey and Julian to sing with her, and gently but swiftly made sure the wound was perfectly clean, then sutured the cut.

'That was brilliant singing, sweetheart,' she told the little boy. She glanced up at Mrs Livesey. 'They're dissolvable stitches, so you don't have to worry about bringing him back to have them taken out. You need to keep an eye on him over the next couple of days; if he starts being sick, has a fit or is drowsy or just a bit unwell and you feel something's not right, come straight back. A mother's instinct is usually pretty sound and you know your child best.' She smiled. 'It's a lot to take in, so I'll give you a leaflet about head injuries.'

'And I have to keep him awake, right?'

'No, it's perfectly safe to let Julian go to sleep— he's going to be tired from crying and the stress of hurting himself. If you're worried, try waking him after about an hour. I can tell you now, he'll be pretty grumpy about it, but that's normal. If you can't wake him easily, that's when you need to bring him back.'

She answered a few more questions and, once Mrs Livesey was reassured, Louisa gave Julian a shiny 'bravery' sticker and called in her next patient.

When she walked into the staff kitchen for a swift coffee break, Dominic was there.

'Good timing. The kettle's hot.' He smiled at her. 'Want a coffee?'

That smile was lethal, Louisa thought. Those dimples…no wonder her heart felt as if it had just done another of those odd little flips. But Dominic was her colleague. There wasn't room in her life for him to be anything more than that. And, even if there was, she'd got it so badly wrong last time that she was wary of repeating her mistake. *Handsome is as handsome does.*

She strove to sound normal. 'Thanks, that'd be wonderful. Milk, no sugar, please.'

'Same as me.' He paused. 'How's the little one you were giving stitches to?'

'He's fine.' She looked at him in surprise. 'How do you know about that?'

'I was passing through Minors earlier, and I heard you singing a magic song.'

She felt herself colour. 'Um.'

'Hey, don't be embarrassed. I'm all in favour of whatever it takes to make a child feel less frightened, and singing's great. I learned three magic tricks when I was a student, precisely so I could make a child concentrate on something other than the reason they came in to see me.'

'Magic tricks?'

He handed her a mug of coffee. 'What's this behind your ear?' He touched her ear briefly; it was the lightest possible contact but it made Louisa very, very aware of him. When he brought his hand away again, he was flourishing a coin between his thumb and index finger—which he then proceeded to flip between his fingers, one by one.

'That's very impressive.'

'It's called a Vegas coin roll,' he told her.

'That's going to beat the offer of a sticker every single time—especially for the boys,' she said with a smile.

'It doesn't take long to learn. I'll teach you some time, if you like,' he said. 'Actually, I was hoping to catch you today. Ric says they have a space, so come along on Saturday for a chat. Any time you like between nine and four—he or Bea will be around.' He fished in his pocket and brought out a folded piece of paper. 'This is their phone number, their address and directions to the stables from the centre of Brighton.'

She really hadn't expected that, and her breath caught. An unexpected kindness. 'Thank you. It'll mean the world to Ty. He's been obsessed with horses for years—but, living in London, we didn't really get to see horses unless we went out at the weekend to one of the farm park places.'

'And you thought that maybe he'd grow out of the obsession, get interested in something else?'

She nodded. 'Our paediatrician said these obsessions are very common with Asperger's children, and they tend to change as the children grow up. But he still really, really loves horses.'

'I'm with him, there. I met my horse when he was an hour old, and I fell in love with him on the spot.'

She could identify with that. The moment she'd first held Tyler, she'd felt a rush of love like nothing she'd ever experienced before—a deep, deep sense of wonder mingled with protective-ness and sheer joy. She knew that some mothers found it took time to bond with their child, but for her it had been instant and overwhelming—and the love had grown even deeper over the years. 'I'd better get back to my patients,' she said. 'And thank you again. I really appreciate it.'

On Saturday morning, Tyler was almost beside himself with excitement. She drove him to the stables, and Bea showed them around.

'Did Dominic mention about...?' Louisa asked quietly when they were in the tack room and Tyler was trying on hard hats.

Bea smiled. 'Yes. I assume he told you about Andy?' At Louisa's blank look, she contin-ued, 'Ric's younger brother. He has Asperger's. Actually, he's in charge of stable management—Ric and I run the classes,' she explained. 'So you don't need to worry. We're aware of the chal-lenges, but as far as I'm concerned if a child loves horses and wants to ride, my job is to help the child do just that. We'll work around the challenges together, because we're all on the same team.'

Louisa had to swallow hard.

Bea patted her on the shoulder. 'Riding's going to be great for him.'

'Will he be in a class?'

'I prefer one to one with beginners, at least for the first couple of months, until they're a bit more confident. But if he wants to come along to a class as well, once we've got him started, that's fine.'

'Dominic said you do RDA work.'

Bea nodded. 'We have half a dozen ponies that we use for RDA sessions—they're very calm and gentle. We run one class each day especially for RDA students. And it's not just about physical therapy, though of course riding's great for improving muscle tone and posture and helping to develop fine and gross motor skills. It's about life skills, too—being with the horses helps both children and adults with communication skills, taking responsibility and being part of a team. And connecting with the animals brings in a new element to their lives.' She paused. 'Really, Louisa, you don't need to worry. We'll take very good care of him. You can come and watch, bring someone with you, or even just sit in the car and read while he's having a lesson. Whatever makes you comfortable.'

'I'd like to watch. Not because I don't trust you,' Louisa hastened to add.

'But because he's your baby and you don't want to miss a thing.' Bea smiled. 'The first time they ride without being on a leading rein, it's like watching them take their first steps. It always makes me tear up as much as their mums.'

And then Louisa realised that Bea would take as good care of Tyler as she would herself; as the tension in her shoulders eased, she realised how worried she'd been.

'He'll be *fine*,' Bea said softly.

Tyler appeared before them, wearing a hard hat. 'It fits, Mum.' He beamed at her.

'Come on. I've got half an hour before my next lesson. Let's get Polo saddled up and you can have a walk round the paddock,' Bea said.

Tyler's eyes went wide. 'Really?'

'Really. Polo's going to be your special horse for a while, so let's get you introduced.'

Watching her son being led round the paddock put a real lump in Louisa's throat. And

Tyler was glowing afterwards. 'I did it, Mum. I'm going to be a knight. Just like the man in the photograph.'

'The man in the photograph?' Louisa was mystified.

Bea looked at her. 'Ah. You didn't know.'

'Know what?'

Bea blew out a breath. 'I feel as if I'm breaking a confidence here. But I guess you need to see it.' She took Louisa and Tyler back to the tack room and showed Louisa the photograph on the wall in silence. A man on a white horse, wearing black armour and carrying a lance.

When Louisa peered more closely at it, she realised that the helmet's visor was up and she could see the rider's face. Someone she recognised. 'Dominic?'

'He still has Pegasus, but he doesn't joust any more,' Bea said.

Dominic was a knight—or, at least, he had been one. But, given that he'd been so open about the fact that he had a horse, and that he'd helped her arrange riding lessons for Tyler, why on earth hadn't he said anything to her when she'd mentioned how much her son wanted to be a knight? 'Why did he give up jousting?' she asked.

'I think it'd be better if he told you,' Bea said. 'It's not my place.'

'Was he hurt?' But she could see the mingled concern and awkwardness on Bea's face. 'Sorry, I shouldn't have asked that. It's not fair to you. Forget I said anything.'

'That's what I want to be. A knight,' Tyler told her.

'A knight on a white charger, hmm?' Louisa asked.

'The horse isn't white, he's grey,' Tyler corrected.

'He looks white to me,' Louisa said.

'White horses are *always* called grey, Mum,' Tyler informed her, rolling his eyes.

She ignored his impatience. In Tyler's mind, if he knew something, it followed that the whole world must know it, too. And in the same painstaking amount of detail.

'He's a Percheron. They come from Normandy in France,' Tyler explained, 'from a place called Le Perche. It's thought that Percherons are descended from destriers, but they're bigger and heavier than the medieval warhorses. Destriers were trained so you didn't have to use the reins, because your hands would be full carrying your sword and your shield.'

'Absolutely right,' Dominic said. 'Hello, Louisa.'

Louisa jumped. 'I didn't hear you come in.'

'Sorry. I didn't mean to startle you.' He looked at Tyler. 'And you must be Tyler. How was your first riding lesson?'

'Brilliant, thank you,' Tyler said politely. He peered at Dominic. 'And you're the knight in the picture, aren't you? Bea says your horse is called Pegasus. That's a cool name. How big is he?'

'Seventeen hands.'

'And how much does he weigh?'

'Nearly nine hundred kilograms.'

Tyler looked serious. 'That's quite a lot.'

'It feels like even more than that if he stands on your foot,' Dominic said with a wry smile.

'Does he live here?'

'Yes.' Dominic paused. 'You can come and see him, if you like—if that's all right with your mum.'

'Please, Mum? Can I?' Tyler's gaze was full of entreaty.

'He's very gentle,' Dominic reassured Louisa.

And *huge*, she thought, when Dominic took them over to the stables.

Tyler duly admired the horse, asking if he was allowed to stroke him and then, at Dominic's agreement, stroking the horse's nose. 'He's beautiful.'

'He certainly is,' Dominic agreed.

'Are you jousting this weekend?'

'No.'

His voice was even, but Louisa noticed the shadows in his eyes. Time to head off her son's line of conversation. 'Ty, we ought to—' she began, but Tyler spoke over her.

'But there's that picture of you. You're a knight. You had a lance and you were wearing armour, so you must be a jouster.'

'Not any more.'

'Why not?'

'Ty, you can't ask questions like that,' Louisa said.

'Why not?'

'It's rude.'

'But I didn't say a swear.'

How was she going to explain this? 'Ty, let's talk about this later, OK?'

'But I *wasn't* rude,' Tyler said, looking puzzled.

Dominic raked a hand through his hair. 'It's a fair question. I don't joust any more because there was an accident and someone got hurt.'

He frowned. 'My mum's a nurse. She makes people better. Why didn't your friend go to see a nurse or a doctor?'

Dominic took a deep breath. 'It doesn't always work that way. Sometimes even a nurse or doctor can't fix things.'

'Oh.' Tyler digested the information. 'Do you miss jousting?'

'Ty, let's talk about something else,' Louisa pleaded. 'I dunno—what the horse eats, what kind of saddle he has?'

But her son refused to budge. 'If I'd been a knight and I didn't do it any more, I think I'd miss jousting,' Tyler said. 'I want to be a knight.'

'It takes a lot of practice and hard work,' Dominic warned.

'I don't mind. I'm going to practise holding the

reins at home. Bea showed me how. All I need is a ribbon.'

'So let's go and buy the ribbon now,' Louisa said, seeing an opening. She caught Dominic's eye and mouthed, 'Sorry.'

He said nothing, and she stifled a sigh. So much for thinking he understood about Asperger's and the way it gave a child tunnel vision. Then again, Ty had obviously trampled on a really sore spot. He hadn't meant to: he just hadn't been able to pick up the visual clues that Dominic was uncomfortable and she hadn't been able to head Tyler in another direction.

'Time to say goodbye, Ty,' she said.

'Goodbye, and thank you for showing me your horse,' Tyler said politely.

Dominic leaned back against the stable door and watched them both walk over the yard. Hell. He hadn't been prepared for that one.

Do you miss jousting?

Yes, he missed it. Missed it like crazy. Holding the lance in his right hand and the reins in his left, then focusing on the tilt, urging Pegasus to a quick canter and then closing in, focusing on where he was going to land his lance. Speed, precision and skill: the kind of thrill that reminded him he was still alive.

Except he'd been a little too precise, the last time he'd jousted. Too fast. And he'd unhorsed his opponent. Oliver had fallen awkwardly, and the armour hadn't been enough to protect his back: he'd ended up with an incomplete spinal injury. An injury that had left him stuck in a wheelchair and ruined his career—because, as a surgeon, you needed strength as well as delicacy. And you also needed to be able to move round your patient. Stand up. Lean over. Oliver couldn't do that any more.

Hell, hell, hell. He'd taken so much away from his brother. His career, his hobbies, his mobility, his *joie de vivre*—Oliver was in too much pain, most of the time, to be full of laughter the way he'd used to be.

So giving up jousting had been the least Dominic could do. To make absolutely sure he never made a mistake like that again and someone else ended up badly hurt.

Pegasus whickered and shoved his head against Dominic's.

'Yeah. I know you miss it, too.' He made a fuss of his horse. 'But we just do steady hacking nowadays, OK? It's safer.'

On Monday, Louisa sought out Dominic at lunchtime. 'I've got something for you.'

'For me?' He looked at her in surprise.

She went over to her locker, took out a plastic wallet and handed it to him.

He looked at it; it was a sketch of a horse. And not just any horse. One he recognised. 'That's Pegasus.'

'Ty drew him for you yesterday. He just wanted to say thank you. For helping me sort out the lessons and for letting him make a fuss of your horse.'

'No worries.' He stared at the picture. 'Nobody's ever drawn my horse for me before. And he did this from memory, from seeing Pegasus just once?' At Louisa's nod, he blew out a breath. 'Wow. He's seriously good at this.'

'I'll tell him you liked it, shall I?' She looked pleased, too; clearly she was more used to people being put off by her son's directness.

'You can tell him I'm going to frame it,' Dominic said. 'And tell him thank you.'

'I'm sorry about the way he grilled you. He didn't mean to trample on a sore spot. He doesn't pick up—'

'Visual cues, and he has tunnel vision,' Dominic finished. 'I know. I'm used to Andy.' Andy had said the same thing, too: Why let the accident stop you jousting? He'd gone further, saying that Dominic giving up jousting wouldn't fix Oliver's back, so he was being completely self-indulgent and wallowing in it.

Maybe Andy and Tyler were right.

But Dominic still couldn't see past the guilt. Oliver would never joust again, or be a surgeon again. And that knowledge was hard enough to live with; harder still was the knowledge that his brother was in constant pain. Oliver had forgiven him, but Dominic still couldn't forgive himself.

'Are you all right?' Louisa asked, looking concerned.

'Old ghosts.' He shook himself. 'Ignore me. I'm fine.'

And that was the biggest fib of all.

* * *

Dominic had gone back into his shell, Louisa thought over the next couple of days. He was always perfectly polite and professional if she was working with him in Resus, but she was aware of his reserve. She tried to put it out of her head; they were colleagues, so it shouldn't matter. As long as the patients were treated properly, it shouldn't matter that he was reserved with her.

And then, on Wednesday evening, her car refused to start after Tyler's riding lesson. 'Oh, great.'

'Why won't your car work, Mum?' Ty asked.

'I don't know, love.' She sighed. 'I'd better call the roadside rescue people.'

She'd been waiting for nearly a quarter of an hour when Bea came over. 'Are you all right?'

'My car won't start. I've called the roadside rescue people—hopefully they'll be here soon and they'll able to fix it.' And hopefully it wouldn't cost a fortune; the expenses of moving had eaten into her savings.

'Come and sit in the kitchen. It's getting chilly out here. I'll get you a coffee,' Bea said, shepherding them inside and switching on the kettle. 'Ty, would you prefer juice or water?'

'Apple juice, please.'

She rummaged in the fridge. 'Sorry, love. I've got orange or cranberry. Or milk.'

'Nothing, thank you.'

'Always so polite. You have beautiful manners, Ty,' she said with a smile.

Tyler was busy drawing a picture of Polo when the roadside rescue people arrived.

'He'll be fine in here with me,' Bea said, ruffling Tyler's hair. 'He knows where you are if he needs you—right, Ty?'

He smiled at her. 'Right.'

When the mechanic had hooked up the diagnostic computer, Dominic came over. In faded jeans, riding boots, a white shirt with the sleeves rolled up and no tie, he looked incredibly touchable. 'What's the problem?'

'Spark plugs,' the mechanic said. 'Two of them. The problem is, they'll need specialist equipment to get them out—they're not a standard size and I don't have the right equipment to sort it out here. The manufacturer changed them on this particular model,' he said, rolling his eyes. 'It's not like the old days, when spark plugs were the same on every car. If just one had gone, I could've disengaged it for you and you would've been safe to get home or to the garage, but with two gone it's not safe to do that, I'm afraid. If you ring the main dealer now, they'll still be there,' he suggested, 'and they'll book you in so I can put your car on the back of the tow truck, and all you have to do is drop your keys through the door in an envelope.'

'Would you be able to drop us home afterwards?' she asked.

'Sorry, love. It's not covered by your policy. I would've bent the rules for you, given that you've got a little one, but I've got another callout waiting,' he said.

'Fair enough. I can call a taxi.'

The dealer's service department was just about to close, but they duly booked her in for the next morning and asked her to drop the keys through their door.

She was about to arrange for a taxi to meet them at the garage when Dominic laid a hand on his arm. 'Don't worry about calling a taxi. I'll follow you to the garage and drop you and Ty home.'

'I can't impose on you like that.'

He shrugged. 'From what Tyler tells me, you don't live that far from me. And I'm finished here for this evening anyway.'

'Actually, I can drop the keys through the letter-box for you at the dealer's,' the mechanic added, 'if that saves a bit of time.'

'And it means you'll get home quicker—Tyler's routine won't be thrown out so much,' Dominic said.

That was the clincher. Ty. Although he coped much better with change nowadays than he had as a small child, it would still throw him. Routine was really, really important to him, and Louisa tried hard to stick to it. 'Thank you. Both of you. That's really kind.'

Louisa clearly wasn't used to leaning on anyone, Dominic thought, so she must've been a single parent for quite a while now. And she'd been adamant about Ty's father not being part of his life. Whatever had happened between them, it had obviously hurt her badly. Not that he could ask. It would be way too tactless.

When he pulled up outside the little terraced house they were renting, Louisa said, 'Would you like to come in and stay for dinner? It's nothing special—just pasta, garlic bread and salad—but you'd be very welcome.'

Tempting. So very, very tempting. He was about to say no when Tyler added, 'If you don't, then Mum will have to buy you flowers to say thank you for helping, and boys don't really like flowers so she'll fuss about it.'

He couldn't help laughing. 'OK, then, thanks. I have to admit, it'll be nice to have home-cooked food for a change.'

'Don't you cook?' Tyler asked.

'Not unless it comes in a packet with instructions for microwaving,' he admitted.

'Tut, and you a doctor,' Louisa teased.

'Can I show you my horse?' Tyler asked, the second Louisa had unlocked the front door. 'I got a commendation for it in Art today at school.'

'Well done.' Louisa gave him a hug and a kiss.

They both admired the drawing.

'Can I show you my other horses?' Tyler asked.

'Sorry,' Louisa mouthed.

'I'd love to see them,' Dominic said, meaning it.

Tyler showed him the drawings, one by one. Dominic was blown away by the detail, both of the horses and of the knights. 'You've got the armour exactly right, too.'

'It's called a harness,' Tyler said, 'but I guess you know that, because you have one.'

'Ye-es.' Not that he'd used it in two years. He hadn't even been able to bring himself to polish it. It was locked away in a trunk.

'Can I come to your house and see it some time?'

Dominic froze. And, just at that moment, Louisa walked into the living room. She'd clearly overheard the last bit because she frowned. 'Tyler, it's rude to invite yourself. And anyway, dinner's ready. Apple juice for everyone?'

Tyler led him into the dining room, which was small but neat. Just like the one in the living room, the mantelpiece was crowded with photographs: Louisa and Tyler, an older man and woman who he assumed were her parents, and a man who looked enough like her that he had to be her brother. Clearly she was close to her family. He'd been close to his, too; but his guilt had driven him away.

'I'd love a suit of armour,' Tyler said as he sat down. 'Grandad and me found a shop that sells suits of armour, when Mum and Nanna went to do girly stuff. Well, *bits* of armour,' he amended. 'I really wanted a cuirass, but it was too big for me and it was a bit expensive. Then we sat on the beach and had chips. And I found a pebble that looks like a horse's head. I'll show you.'

He rushed up to his room before Louisa could stop him.

She grimaced. 'Sorry. He's a bit impulsive.'

'I think most eight-year-old boys are,' he said. 'I know Oliver and I used to drive our mum crazy. He's a nice kid. And he's brilliant at drawing.'

Tyler rushed back in with the pebble, and Dominic duly admired it.

Dinner was simple but good; though it felt odd, being almost like part of a family.

'How was your day, Dominic?' Tyler asked.

The question really surprised him; but then he realised this was probably part of the evening routine; obviously Louisa was gently training her son in the art of social niceties to make his life easier as he grew older, just as Andy's parents had done with him.

'It was good, thanks,' he said. 'I patched up someone who fell off his bike and helped someone else whose heart stopped working properly.'

'What was the best bit?' Tyler asked, looking serious.

Dominic thought about it. 'Going to the stables. How about you?'

'My day was good. I got a commendation in Art, but the stables was the best bit. I like the smell of horses. And Polo's hair is all soft, except his mane, and that's like Mum's hair when we've gone swimming and it dries all frizzy at the ends.'

Dominic couldn't help smiling. 'Does yours go frizzy?'

'No, because my hair's short.' Tyler looked at him and frowned. 'But yours isn't, so yours must go frizzy, too.'

'I haven't been swimming for a long time.'

'You could come with us. We go on Thursday nights. And then we have fish and chips at Nanna and Grandad's. You could come with us tomorrow, if you like.'

'Sweetheart, Dominic's probably busy,' Louisa cut in.

'Sorry, your mum's right,' Dominic said. 'But maybe another time.' And, to his surprise, he realised that he meant it. It wasn't just politeness. He really would like to go swimming with them, then eat fish and chips out of the wrapper.

And the realisation that he wanted to get involved was even scarier. He should be wanting to run a mile: Louisa wasn't the kind of woman who wanted just a fling, and she came as a package. She was nothing like the women he used to date, who tended to be tall, leggy, blonde and exquisitely dressed. And yet she drew him far more than any of those women had. He wasn't sure what it was: her warmth; her selflessness; the way she treated everyone with kindness and courtesy? All he knew was that he wanted to get to know her better.

When they'd finished their meal, Louisa shooed Tyler upstairs for a bath.

'And I ought to go,' Dominic said. 'Can I help with the washing up first?'

'No, it's fine. It won't take me two minutes.'

'If you're sure.' He called up the stairs, 'See you at the stables, Ty.'

'Bye,' the little boy called back.

'Thank you,' he said as Louisa walked with him to the front door. 'I've enjoyed this evening.' He bent to kiss her cheek, but he misjudged it and somehow ended up kissing her on the mouth. It was the briefest, briefest touch, but it made his mouth tingle.

He pulled back sharply. 'I'd better go. See you tomorrow at work.'

'See you tomorrow,' she echoed.

When Louisa had closed the door behind him, she stood there for a while, just touching her mouth. It was the first time she'd been kissed by a man other than her father, son or brother for a long, long time; and the first time in years that she'd felt such a zing of attraction.

She liked Dominic. A lot. She liked the way he worked, the way he cared for his patients, the way he treated all his colleagues with respect, no matter how junior they were. The way he noticed if a student was struggling and would spend time afterwards explaining what he'd done and why—and she'd just bet he did exactly the same thing at the stables. He was patient with Ty without being patronising, and took Ty's quirks in his stride.

Not to mention the fact that he was spine-tinglingly gorgeous, too.

It would be very, very easy to fall for Dominic Hurst. But she had Tyler to think about. He was still young, and he needed more consideration than the average child; he found talking about emotions difficult, and was much happier with facts and figures.

So she'd better be sensible and keep things strictly professional between herself and Dominic. Anything more would be risking heartache—and not just for herself. This wasn't going to happen.

CHAPTER FOUR

DOMINIC had visions of Louisa all the way home, with her hair loose spreading over the water like a mermaid's; he'd just bet that she was a graceful swimmer. And he was cross with himself for not being able to get her out of his head. This was crazy. He didn't have room for a relationship in his life. He'd made sure of that, filling his time with work and his horse. When he wasn't at the hospital, he was at the stables. He went on team nights out with his colleagues, because he knew it was good for staff morale and helped to build solid working relationships; but he didn't do relationships. Before Oliver's accident, he'd never met anyone who'd tempted him to settle down—he'd been happy to keep his relationships light and just for fun. After the accident, he'd avoided personal relationships, not wanting to let anyone else down the way he'd let his family down.

Louisa Austin was different.

What was it about her that drew him so much? It wasn't just the way she was at work—kind, efficient and professional with patients and colleagues alike. And it wasn't just the way she was so selfless with her son. There was a calmness about her, a warmth, that made him want to stop driving himself so hard and just *be*.

He'd made a bad mistake, kissing her like that.

Admittedly, it hadn't been a passionate kiss. But it had been more than the friendly peck on the cheek he'd intended. And the softness, the sweetness of her mouth against his…it had made him want more. So much more.

'It's not going to happen. There are too many complications. We're just colleagues,' he told himself firmly.

But even so, he found himself seeking her out at lunchtime the next day. 'Can I steal some of your lunch break for a quick debriefing?' he asked.

'Sure.'

To his relief, she wasn't wary with him. So he might not have spoiled things between them completely.

'So which patient are we talking about?' she

asked when they were sitting in a quiet corner of the hospital cafeteria.

'Um, not a patient exactly. I wanted to talk to you without half the ward as an audience—to apologise about last night.' He could feel his skin growing warm.

'It's OK. I know you didn't mean anything by it,' she said.

It had been accidental. But he couldn't take his eyes off her mouth. Which was crazy. He knew that neither of them was in the right place for a relationship. And he didn't do relationships, not since Oliver's accident. Nothing had changed.

But Louisa still drew him. He wanted to kiss her some more. Properly, this time.

He pulled himself together with difficulty. 'What did the garage say about your car?'

'They've got to order in a part. It should be done tomorrow.'

'I can give you a lift home tonight, if you like.' The words were out before he could stop them. But he could see on her face that she was going to say no.

'Thanks for the offer, but I can't make you go out of your way.'

This was where he should be relieved at the get-out, but his mouth was on a roll. 'It's not really out of my way. I have to go right past your place to get to the stables from here.'

'I need to pick up Ty from after-school club first.'

School was nearby, too. 'Not a problem.'

'Then thank you.' She looked relieved. 'I was going to ask Mum to bail me out, but I hate having to rely on my parents—it's not fair to them, asking them to help.'

'I'm sure they don't mind. And you seem pretty independent to me.'

'I try to be.'

He noticed that she turned the conversation away from herself after that; she was as cagey as he was.

But for some crazy reason he found himself smiling all afternoon.

When they met Tyler at school, the little boy seemed delighted to see him. 'Does this mean you're coming swimming with us tonight?' he asked.

'Sorry, I don't have my swimming things with

me. I'm just giving you and your mum a lift home because her car's still being fixed.'

'We're going to take the bus to the pool and then Nanna and Grandad are going to meet us there,' Louisa explained.

'But you will come swimming with us another time?' Tyler asked.

'We'll see,' Dominic said, glancing at Louisa; her expression was unreadable.

'That's grown-up speak for "No",' Tyler said with a sigh.

'No, it means I don't make promises unless I'm absolutely sure I can keep them,' Dominic said. 'If I'm treating a patient, I can't suddenly stop just because it's the end of my shift. And that means sometimes I'm late for things or I don't manage to get there at all. And I don't like disappointing people, so I don't make many promises.' He smiled at the little boy as he pulled up outside Louisa's house. 'See you later—enjoy your swim.'

'Are you going to the stables now?'

'I am indeed.'

'Give Pegasus a pat for me,' Tyler said, scrambling out of the car. 'And thank you for bringing us home.'

'Pleasure.' The little boy was so earnest and always so polite; he found it touching.

'And thanks for being so patient,' Louisa added quietly. 'I do try to limit his questions. But I can't keep telling him off in front of people—it's not his fault that he finds social cues so hard.'

'He's a nice kid,' Dominic said. 'And you're doing a great job.'

He was still thinking about her when he was grooming Pegasus. 'The problem is,' he told his horse, 'I really like her. I like everything about her. She's bright, she's warm and kind, she's good with patients and staff alike. And she's gorgeous. Well, hey, you've seen her. Her mouth's like a rosebud, her eyes are the clear grey of a winter sky, and—'

'You're waxing a bit poetic there,' Ric said.

Dominic blew out a breath. 'Thanks for nearly making me stick the hoofpick into my hand! Why are you creeping about the stables?'

'I wasn't creeping. You didn't hear me because your attention was focused…' Ric coughed '…elsewhere.'

Dominic grimaced. 'Well, thanks.'

'You were describing Louisa, I take it? She's nice.'

'And she has commitments.'

'Tyler, you mean?' Ric was utterly relentless. 'You get on well with him. I've seen you. So the problem is…?'

'She's not the type to do a casual relationship.'

'So try having a proper relationship for a change,' Ric suggested.

Dominic shook his head. 'That's not what I want.'

'Isn't it?'

Dominic didn't want to think about it, let alone answer the question, so he continued grooming his horse.

'It's time you forgave yourself,' Ric said softly.

'What if I let her down?' The question slipped out before Dominic could stop it.

But Ric didn't seem fazed at all. Didn't back away. Didn't make a big deal out of it. 'What if you don't?' he countered. 'Look at what you do every day. Do you let your patients down? No. If anything, you push yourself harder to make sure you don't. Do you let anyone down at the stables? No.'

'I don't have room in my life for a relation-ship.'

'Of course you do. If she deserves you, she'll understand you and you'll work out some kind of compromise. Just like Bea and me.'

'It's complicated.'

'You'd be bored with something easy.'

Dominic sighed. 'Have you got an answer for everything?'

'Yup. And if I haven't, Bea has.' Ric paused. 'Look, I've seen you together. You like her and she likes you. And you've got work in common— she'll understand about your job not being nine to five. Her son loves horses, so she'll understand that side of you, too.'

'It's a bad idea to mix work and pleasure.'

Ric ignored him. 'What's the worst that can happen? She'll say no? Then you can still be friends.' He regarded his friend. 'But I think she'd be good for you. She might teach you to be kind to yourself.'

'As you've known me since we were both in

nappies,' Dominic said, 'I'll forget you said that.'

'Because I've known you that long, I'm about the only person who could say it to you.' Ric gave him a searching look. 'Except maybe for someone who's known you a teensy bit longer. Who worries about you, too.'

Dominic frowned. 'Have you been talking about me?'

'If someone rings me when I'm up to my eyes in paperwork and in a filthy mood,' Ric said, 'then I'm not really responsible for my mouth running away with me.'

Dominic narrowed his eyes. 'Mum or Oliver?'

'Irrelevant.'

'Oliver,' Dominic guessed, 'otherwise I would've had a parental summons to Sunday lunch and general smothering. What did you say?'

Ric sighed. 'Just that I agreed with him. That it's time you let people back into your life.'

'Don't be ridiculous. Of course I let people into my life.'

'Let people close, then. Someone besides your family, me and Bea. And Pegasus agrees with us—don't you, boy?'

The horse whickered.

Dominic grimaced. 'Traitor.'

'We're worried about you,' Ric said. 'Because we love you. So just ask her, will you?'

'Yeah, yeah. If I get time.'

But Dominic thought about it a lot, over the next few days. Days during which the more he saw of Louisa, the more attracted he was to her. Just as he'd admitted to Ric, she was warm, she was kind, she was great with people. And those serious grey eyes drew him. Particularly when they were lit with laughter.

And maybe his best friend had a point.

'It's the team night out on Friday. Ten-pin bowling. Are you coming?' Essie asked on the Monday morning.

'I'm not sure yet,' Louisa hedged.

'If you can't get a babysitter, Ty could come and watch a film with my lot. They're going to have pizza, so he's very welcome.'

'Thanks for the offer, but—' Louisa began.

Essie patted her arm. 'It would do you good to have an evening out, plus it's good for team-building. Even Dominic always turns up to team nights out.'

The idea of seeing Dominic outside work, and not just at the stables—oh, help. But Louisa duly rang her parents that evening. 'Mum, I hate to ask, but there's a team night out on Friday and Essie asked me to go—I wondered if you could come over and sit with Ty for a couple of hours, if you're not already doing—?'

'Going out with your workmates would do you good,' Gillian cut in firmly. 'Of course we'll have Ty—he can have a sleepover at ours, and you can pick him up before his riding lesson on Saturday.'

'Thanks, Mum. I owe you.'

'Nonsense.' Gillian sighed. 'You're too independent, you know.'

'I don't want you to feel I'm taking you for granted.'

Gillian tutted. 'Don't be so silly. Of course you don't take us for granted. We love spending time with our grandson. I'd be very happy for you to ask me to babysit more often.'

Particularly, Louisa thought, if a date was involved. It was one of her mother's favourite subjects: how it was long past time that Louisa put Jack behind her and started dating again. Not that she intended to be drawn on that one. 'Thanks, Mum,' she said.

On the Friday lunchtime, Dominic said casually, 'I'm giving Ronnie and Jess a lift to the bowling place. So there's a spare seat in my car if you'd like a lift, too.'

'Thank you. That'd be nice.'

'So are you a demon bowler, Louisa?' Ronnie asked as they walked into the centre later that evening.

'I'm afraid I'm absolutely hopeless,' Louisa said. 'I've been about half a dozen times in my life—always for work, and I always come last.'

'We'll stick you on Dominic's team, then,' Ronnie said with a grin. 'That'll bring his average down and give the rest of us a chance.'

Dominic scoffed. 'I'm not that good.'

But he turned out to be brilliant. He scored strike after strike after strike. And, when Louisa had her third frame in a row without knocking down a single pin because her ball had gone straight into the gutter, he disappeared briefly. By his return, two barriers had sprung up between the bowling lane and the gutter.

'That's cheating,' Aiden, one of the junior doctors, informed him.

'No, it isn't. The bumper bars are up on your lane, too, and Ronnie's a genius at zig-zag bowling,' Dominic retorted. 'So your team has just got an advantage.'

Louisa flushed when she realised what he'd done: now there was no way she could fail to knock down at least one pin. 'I feel like a baby.'

'No, it's to do with confidence,' Dominic said. 'Once you realise you can do it, you won't need the bars up.' He walked with her to the line when it was her next turn. 'It's a bit like tennis—your finishing position affects where the ball goes. Your last three frames, you ended up too far to the left, so try either finishing with your hand straight in the middle, or start off aiming very slightly to the right. Like this.' He stood behind her and guided her arm very gently.

Louisa was incredibly aware of the warmth of his body; she wished now that she'd worn a thick sweater instead of a strappy T-shirt, because she could feel her body reacting to his touch. Hopefully, as it was a special 'glow bowling' evening and all the lights were down except over the bowling lane itself, nobody else would notice the physical signs of her arousal.

'You can do this,' he said. 'It's like learning to put a line in. The first few times, when you practise on an orange, you don't think you'll ever be able to do it to a real, live person. And then suddenly it clicks, and after the first couple of times you do it in Resus, you wonder why on earth you thought you couldn't do it.'

'I suppose so.'

She did as he suggested, and to her delight she knocked three pins down.

'High five, sister,' he said with a grin, clapping his palm against hers.

She knocked another three down on her next go—again without her ball even touching the bumper bar.

'See? Leave them up until you're really confident, but you can definitely do it,' he said. 'All you needed was to believe in yourself.'

Her score still wasn't brilliant at the end of the

night, but it was a personal best; and Louisa knew it was all thanks to Dominic.

After they'd eaten at the American diner next to the bowling alley, Dominic dropped off Jess and Ronnie, then drove to Louisa's house.

'Would you like to come in for coffee?' she asked.

How could he resist the chance to spend just a little longer with her? 'Thanks. That'd be nice.' But the house seemed silent when she opened the door. 'I thought you said your parents were babysitting?' he asked.

'They are. Tyler's staying with them tonight,' she explained.

Which meant that he and Louisa were alone.

And they could talk without worrying that what they said might be overheard or misconstrued.

He followed her into the kitchen and leaned against the table, watching her as she switched the kettle on and shook instant coffee into two mugs. Her movements were so graceful. She fascinated him.

'I enjoyed tonight,' he said.

'Me, too.' She busied herself adding milk, then finally pouring on the hot water.

'Louisa.' He walked over to her and took her hand. 'I might be speaking out of turn, here, but I can't get you out of my head. There's something about you that just draws me. And I'd like to start seeing you.'

Her eyes went wide. 'Dominic. I…' She shook her head. 'I don't date.'

'Because of Tyler? I already know you come as a package. And I'm certainly not expecting you to get babysitters so you can see me. I like your son and I think he likes me—so I'd like to get to know you *both* better. We'll take it as slowly as you like.'

She bit her lip. 'I haven't dated anyone since my marriage broke up.'

He needed to know. 'Very long ago?'

'Five years—Ty was three.'

'Your ex met someone else?' Dominic guessed.

'No.' She closed her eyes for a moment, then lifted her chin; whatever had happened, clearly it was a huge, huge thing for her. 'You know the "terrible twos"? Ty had them really, really badly. We didn't realise at the time that he had Asperger's. He couldn't tell us how he felt, why he needed everything to be in order—so he'd just scream. Most of the time it was something we couldn't do anything about…and he'd scream and he'd scream and he'd scream.' She sighed. 'Jack couldn't cope with the tantrums. And when the nursery suggested we see someone, and the GP referred us to a paediatrician who told us that Ty has Asperger's…he couldn't handle that his son was a bit different.'

Dominic was truly shocked. 'Jack left you because Tyler has Asperger's?'

'He couldn't deal with it.' She sucked in a breath. 'I might as well tell you the rest of it. Ty looks nothing like Jack—he takes after my side of the family. And Jack asked me if Tyler was actually his.'

Dominic couldn't quite take it in. 'He accused you of having an affair?'

She closed her eyes. 'I *didn't* have an affair.'

'That goes without saying.' He realised his fists were clenched, and deliberately splayed his fingers. Apart from the fact that he had no idea where Louisa's ex lived, breaking the man's jaw wouldn't make things any better. 'You're not the type to cheat. What on earth made him think that?'

'It took me a long while to work it out.' She opened her eyes again. 'I think he just wanted to be able to blame the genes on someone else. I'm glad that Ty didn't inherit his father's personality. Though Jack wasn't like that when I met him. I'm not that lousy a judge of character—at least, I don't think I am.'

'You're not,' Dominic said. 'But you see the good in people.' She saw the good in him. 'What about his parents? Surely they…?' His voice faded as he saw her expression tighten.

'They sided with Jack. Which is why Tyler only knows one set of grandparents—*my* parents.' Her gaze connected with his. 'Don't get me wrong, I'm not telling you a sob story; I'm simply trying to explain why I don't date. Because I'm never going to put my son in a position where he can be rejected again.'

'I can understand that.' He shook his head in disgust. 'What kind of person would reject their own child? That's beyond me.'

'Me, too.'

'You're both better off without him.'

She gave him a wry smile. 'You're telling me. I fell out of love with him the moment he told me why he was leaving. That's why I reverted to my maiden name—and I changed Tyler's at the same time.'

'And your ex didn't mind?' No way would Dominic ever have let himself be cut out of his child's life.

'He didn't want us,' she said simply. 'It made life easier for him, because he could pretend he'd never had a child. So now you understand why I have to say no.'

'I understand why you want to say no,' he said. 'But I'm so aware of you. And sometimes I catch your eye at work or at the stables and I think it's the same for you, too. There's chemistry between us.'

'Yes,' she admitted with a sigh. 'But I can't possibly act on it.'

Though she hadn't loosened her hand from his. Which was a good sign. He drew her hand up to his mouth and kissed the back of it, very gently. 'I like you, Louisa. And I happen to like your son. He's got a good heart and he's kind. Yes, he's very direct and he'll only talk about what he's interested in—if you try and head him off, he'll change the subject right back. Some people would find that hard to deal with, but I'm used to that already because of Andy. It doesn't worry me.'

Her eyes were very clear. 'Tyler likes you.'

'Good.' He paused. And she'd admitted that she was attracted to him. 'This thing between you and me—how about we keep it just between us, see where it takes us? And, as far as everyone else is concerned, we're just good friends.'

'You mean, have a secret affair?'

'No,' he said. 'I don't mean anything tawdry or hole-in-the-corner. I mean we'll keep it to ourselves until we're sure what we're doing and we're ready to let other people know that we're seeing each other.'

'Did she hurt you that much?'

He frowned. 'Who?'

'The woman who's made you wary of relationships.'

He shook his head. 'It isn't what you think. I used to be—well, I guess I had a bit of a reputation. All my relationships were short and sweet, just for fun, but it was always mutual. I simply never met anyone who made me want to change that and settle down. And then...' Then he'd caused his brother to end up in a wheelchair. Everything had seemed different after that. 'Life changed,' he said, knowing it was way too succinct but not quite ready to tell her the rest. 'I decided to focus on my career. Except now I've met you, and I can't get you out of my head. And you make me want to try to be...' He paused, trying to think of the right word. 'Different.'

'Different, how?' she asked. 'What's wrong with you as you are?'

A million things, Dominic thought. 'It's complicated. And I don't really want to talk about it right now.' He knew he was being unreasonable; she'd opened up to him, so he ought to do the same with her. But this was all so new. He wanted her to know him better before he told her about Oliver.

'So this is just between you and me.'

This time, he knew, she wasn't saying no. 'Just between you and me,' he echoed softly. He kissed the inside of her wrist, and his mouth tingled at the contact. He knew it affected her the same way, because he felt the shiver running through her. 'Louisa.'

She cupped his face with her free hand. 'I'm out of practice at this.'

'That makes two of us.' He turned his head so he could kiss her palm.

'Dominic…'

And then he was kissing her properly. A sweet, tender, exploring kiss that left them both shaking.

A tear slid down her face when he broke the kiss.

'Don't cry, honey.' He wiped away the tear with the pad of his thumb.

'I just…never expected this.'

'Neither did I. Work and the stables were going to be my life. Until you walked into the restroom. That's why I was so rude to you—it threw me,' he said.

'I thought you were being all formal and unapproachable.'

'No. I was trying to keep some distance between us because there was this huge zing of attraction and I really, really didn't want to fall for you.'

'Distance.' She gave him a pointed look, because his arms were still wrapped tightly round her.

'Epic fail.' He kissed her again. 'And *that* was because I need the practice.'

She laughed back. 'That's the worst excuse I've ever heard.' And then, just when he thought she was going to wriggle out of his arms, she kissed him.

Her mouth was sweet and soft and incredibly sensual, and that kiss blew his mind.

When she broke the kiss, he released her and took a step back. 'Distance,' he said. 'Because, even though I want to kiss you until neither of us can think straight, that's not a good idea. I'm not taking anything for granted, and we're most definitely not going to rush this. We're taking this slowly.'

'Agreed.' She handed him a mug of coffee, and lifted her own mug in a toast. 'To taking things slowly.'

'And seeing where it takes us. And keeping it just between us, until we're ready.'

Over the next couple of weeks, Dominic and Louisa snatched coffee breaks or lunch breaks together at work, getting to know each other; and they saw each other more out of work, too. Dominic gave in to Tyler's request to join their swimming session, one Thursday evening, even though he knew it meant meeting her parents—which made everything feel much more serious.

'Mum, Dad, this is Dominic Hurst—our friend,' Louisa introduced them. 'He works with me at the hospital, and he sometimes works with Ty at the stables.'

Dominic was half expecting a grilling about his intentions towards Louisa, but Gillian and Matt Austin turned out to be absolutely lovely, and he found himself relaxing with them, to the point where he accepted the invitation to join them for fish and chips following the swimming session—and insisted on helping to wash up afterwards.

He wasn't quite ready for Louisa to meet his family—there was a lot he needed to tell her, first—but he did invite her and Tyler back to his flat for a pizza one evening.

'Is that my picture?' Tyler asked, spying the framed sketch on the wall.

Dominic smiled. 'You bet it is. It's a brilliant picture.'

The little boy seemed to swell with pride. 'I drew Pegasus from memory.' He glanced around the room. 'Do you keep your harness here?'

He'd known the little boy would ask that, given that Tyler had already drawn a copy of the photograph of him in his jousting kit, along with several other suits of armour. He'd even unlocked the box for the first time in months and checked that the plate hadn't rusted, so he wouldn't disappoint the boy. 'Yes. Want to see it?' he asked.

'Oh, cool!' The little boy's eyes were round with pleasure. Then he glanced at his mother, who'd raised an eyebrow. 'I mean, yes, please.'

His enthusiasm made it easy for Dominic to unlock the box.

'Oh, wow, that's amazing. I've only ever seen silver armour, even at museums,' Tyler said. He smiled. 'Black armour's right for you. Like Edward the Black Prince. He was a champion jouster. Are you?'

'I used to be.' When life had been different. But he didn't want to talk about that. Time for more distraction. 'Want to try it on?'

'Can I? Really?'

'It'll be a bit big for you,' Dominic warned, 'but sure. I'll be your squire and help you put it on. Did you know there are twenty-seven pieces in a set?'

Tyler nodded. 'And the squire used to clean the armour with sand and vinegar. Do you know what they had to use if they didn't have any vinegar?' He glanced at his mother, then whispered gleefully in Dominic's ear, 'They used wee!'

Dominic couldn't help laughing. 'That's gross, Ty!'

'I saw it on telly. And I looked it up in a book afterwards, so I know it's true.'

Just what Dominic would have done himself, at that age. Still smiling, he helped Tyler put most of the armour on.

'Wow, it's heavy.'

'Because it's eighteen-gauge steel,' Dominic told him.

'Look, Mum, I'm a real knight,' Tyler said when Dominic finished putting the armour on him, clearly delighted.

'Do you mind if I…?' Louisa waved her mobile

phone at Dominic, obviously keen to take a photograph of her son.

'Sure.'

'Are you going to wear your armour again?' Tyler asked when Dominic had packed it away.

'I don't know,' Dominic said.

'Ty, you need to wash your hands before tea,' Louisa reminded him. As the little boy scampered out to the bathroom, she said quietly, 'Sorry about that.'

'I should've anticipated the question. And I could've lied and told him I didn't have my harness any more.'

'But you don't lie.'

'No, I don't.' Except for a lie of omission. He still hadn't told her about the accident. He closed the lid of the trunk. 'The pizza should be here any minute. Let's go and sit down.'

'Is this your family?' Tyler asked, looking at the photographs on the mantelpiece.

'My parents and my elder brother, Oliver,' Dominic said. The photograph was just over two years old. When Oliver had still been at the top of his game, a brilliant surgeon and a brilliant horseman. Guilt flooded through him.

'Mum's got a brother, too. I'd like a brother,' Tyler said reflectively. 'Or a little sister, even.'

Dominic glanced at Louisa, who'd gone very still.

Tyler shrugged. 'But I guess Mum would have to get married before she could have a baby.'

'I'm fine as I am,' Louisa said, though her voice sounded slightly hollow. 'Those are nice dogs.'

Dominic recognised the distraction technique for what it was.

And, to his relief, it worked. 'They're way cool.' Tyler looked longingly at the photograph. 'I'd love a puppy. A wolfhound puppy. That's what a knight would have.'

'We can't have a dog while we're renting. But if we buy a house next year, we might be able to have a dog,' Louisa said, ruffling his hair. 'But not a wolfhound. Something smaller.'

'Absolutely. Having lived with a big dog, I can tell you, if a Great Dane sneaks upstairs and settles on your bed in the crook of your knees, you always end up on the floor when he stretches out. Fudge here is a nightmare for pushing you out of bed,' Dominic said lightly, and to his relief the strain in Louisa's eyes eased.

Well, now he knew what Tyler wanted. A house with a garden, a dog, and a family.

But what did Louisa want? And—at heart—what did *he* really want?

Yet he knew he wasn't quite ready to find out the answers.

CHAPTER FIVE

THE following day found Louisa in Minors.

'I think I've got something in my eye,' Tim Kershaw, her patient, said.

Given how red and inflamed his eye was, she was fairly sure he was right.

'I did rinse my eye out, but it feels like I've got a boulder in there,' he added with a grimace.

A few questions elicited the information that he worked on a building site and he'd forgotten to put protective goggles on. To her relief, he didn't wear contact lenses and he wasn't allergic to any medication. 'What I need to do is have a close look at your eye,' she said. 'I'm going to put some drops in—they'll sting a bit, but then it'll stop hurting and I can examine you properly.'

Though the examination showed her nothing. 'I'm going to need to put some dye in your eye,' she said, 'to show up if there are any scratches. If whatever went into your eye left a scratch behind, it'll feel as if there's something still in there, even though it's gone.'

'I'm in your hands.'

The dye showed her exactly what she'd suspected. 'You've got a corneal abrasion,' she said. 'It'll clear up in a few days, but I'm going to prescribe you some antibiotic ointment and some painkillers. And I need you to wear an eye patch until you get the sensation back in your eye, otherwise you'll risk getting something else in it and you won't feel it so it could cause a lot more damage.'

When she'd finished fitting the eye patch, Tim smiled at her. 'Thanks. I already feel a lot better.' He paused, and his gaze flicked to her left hand. 'Um, can I take you for a drink tonight, to say thank you?'

'There's no need,' Louisa said with a smile. 'It's my job.'

'OK—as a way of getting to know you, then?'

Louisa kept the polite, professional smile on her face. 'It's very sweet of you to ask, but I can't.'

'Because I'm a patient and you're a nurse?' Tim

guessed. 'But when I leave here, I won't be your patient any more.'

'It's not that,' Louisa said, thinking of Dominic. 'I'm already involved with someone. And it's pretty serious.'

Dominic, who was walking through Minors on his way to Reception, heard every single word. And he wondered just who Louisa had meant. Her son? Or—his heart skipped a beat—him? Over the last couple of weeks, the three of them had grown closer. He and Louisa had held hands at the cinema while Tyler had been glued to the screenplay, then gone out for a pizza and talked about their favourite bits of the film. They'd gone for long walks, crunching through autumn leaves while Tyler searched for conkers, or looking for unusual pebbles on the beach. And then there had been the afternoon when they'd gone to the pool and he'd raced Tyler, giving the little boy a head start. 'Because I'm bigger than you, so it takes me fewer strokes to get to the end, and I've been swimming for a lot longer than you have. Giving you a head start makes it fair—it's not me patronising you,' he'd explained. 'And if you beat me, it isn't because I've let you win: it's because you swam better than I did.'

He'd beaten Tyler the first two times. Just by a couple of strokes; although he hadn't wanted to patronise the little boy, he also hadn't wanted to wreck Tyler's confidence. And then he'd spent a quarter of an hour teaching Tyler how to breathe more efficiently between strokes, praising him for trying hard and gently correcting him until he'd got it right.

On their very last race, the little boy had beaten him by a single hand, and Dominic had whooped, lifted him up and spun him round in a victory dance.

Louisa had been close to tears. And, later that evening, she'd held him tightly. 'What you did today…that meant a lot to Tyler.'

'Me, too,' he'd admitted. 'I enjoyed it.' Though he hadn't examined his feelings too closely. They were too new, too far out of his experience, for him to want to analyse them.

Since that afternoon, they'd actually hugged each other goodbye in front of Tyler. And their goodbye kisses when he saw Louisa home after a team night out were starting to linger.

Pretty serious?

Maybe.

Though he was still far from ready to go public.

Apart from anything else, he hadn't told her about Oliver. And he knew he really had to tell her. Sooner, rather than later.

'Mum's found something way cool to do at half-term,' Tyler told Dominic at the stables on Saturday afternoon.

Dominic looked up from where he was cleaning his saddle. 'What's that?'

'We're going to see the jousting at Amberhurst Castle.' Tyler hopped from one foot to the other. 'I can't wait! Do you want to come with us? There's room in Mum's car.'

Oh, hell. How could he have forgotten? The last joust of the season, in the October half-term holidays, just before the ground started getting too boggy from the rain or too hard from the frosts.

Well, he hadn't actually forgotten. He'd deliberately blanked it from his mind. Especially as the joust hadn't been held at Amberhurst for the last two years.

'Thanks for inviting me, but I can't make it,' he said. 'Though you'll have a great time. There's always a re-enactment group camping in the castle grounds on the medieval weekends. You'll see the smith making the armour and the horseshoes; that's always good to watch.'

'Did you ever joust there?' Tyler asked.

Dominic shifted uncomfortably. 'Yes.' More than that, Amberhurst was his family home. He really had to get round to telling Louisa that; but he was trying to choose his words carefully. And there were other things he needed to tell her first.

'So you know the people who are jousting?' Tyler asked.

There was no point in lying. 'Yes.'

'And you jousted against them?'

'Yes.'

'Did you win?'

This was torture. Why hadn't Louisa got her usual second sense and come to the rescue? But she was chatting to Bea, with her back to him. 'Usually,' Dominic said, not wanting to push the little boy away but, at the same time, desperately needing a change of subject.

'So why don't you start jousting again?' Tyler asked. 'I know you said someone got hurt, but jousting's really safe now. It's not like when Henry the Second was killed by splinters from a lance going through his eye into his brain.'

'Back in 1559, you mean? I'm not *quite* that old,' Dominic said wryly.

But Tyler's focus was elsewhere. 'They have rubber bits on the end of the lances, and the end bit's made of really soft wood, so it splinters easily and absorbs some of the impact energy. And knights have better helmets now, the frog-shaped ones so they can see through the slit when they lean forward, but they sit up at the last minute to stop the splinters coming through.'

Dominic couldn't help smiling at Tyler's earnestness. The boy had certainly read up about the subject. But how could he answer the question without dragging up things he'd rather not talk about? 'Ty, I know this sounds like a cop-out, but sometimes grown-up things are complicated.'

'Grown-ups make things *too* complicated,' Tyler said. 'If you miss jousting, and your friends who do jousting miss you, it's obvious that you should do it again. Then everyone will be happy.'

If only it were that simple. Dominic sighed. 'I'll think about it, OK? I'm not making any promises.'

'Any promises for what?' Louisa asked, coming over to them.

'I asked Dominic if he'd come to Amberhurst with us, but he's busy,' Tyler said. 'And he says he'll think about jousting again.'

'About time too,' Andy said, coming in to the tack room and clearly overhearing the tail end of the conversation.

'Hmm. Well, I have a horse to see to,' Dominic said, regardless of the fact that he hadn't finished cleaning his tack. He needed some space. 'Catch you later.'

He thought about it for the rest of the day.

Jousting.

He'd missed it, badly. The speed and the thrill. And if Oliver could bear to have the jousting at Amberhurst again…would seeing his brother back in the saddle rub extra salt in his wounds? Or did he, like Andy, think that Dominic's sacrifice was self-indulgent and pointless?

There was only one way to find out.

When Dominic got home, later that afternoon, he picked up the phone and called his brother.

'You're jousting at Amberhurst?' Louisa asked, surprised.

'Yes.'

'But—I thought you didn't joust any more. What changed your mind?'

'Certain people nagged me about it.'

She bit her lip. 'Tyler?'

'He wasn't the only one.' Dominic looked at her. 'How would you feel about me borrowing your son for part of the day?'

'You're going to take him jousting? When Tyler tells me there's a closing speed of *seventy miles an hour*?' She couldn't help her voice squeaking.

'Of course not. He's a novice rider—no way is he ready to handle a lance,' he reassured her. 'No, I just wondered if he'd like to be my page and hold my standard when I'm on the field.' He smiled. 'Actually, I've got a pretty good idea what his answer would be if I asked him. But I wanted to run the idea past you, first, to see how you felt about it.'

How did she feel about it? Panicky, fearful that her little boy could get hurt. But she also knew that it would do wonders for his confidence and his social skills, so she wouldn't stand in his way. And she appreciated the fact that Dominic had been thoughtful enough to take her feelings into consideration and ask her first. 'He'd be thrilled to bits. But that's all he'd have to do, hold your standard?'

'And give Pegasus a good-luck pat. Andy's going to be my squire for the day and check my armour; Tyler will be perfectly safe with him, staying next to the lances at the side of the tilting ground. He won't be anywhere near the horses—or the splinters when the lances make a strike.'

It was as if he'd zeroed in on her fears and answered them all. 'I don't know what to say.'

'Yes would be a good start. Oh, and that also means that you won't need to get a ticket for the event. You'll both be my guests.'

She shook her head. 'That's too generous.'

'Actually, it's entirely selfish,' he said. 'Because this will be the first time I've jousted since...' His voice caught.

'Since the accident?' All she knew about it was

that someone had been physically hurt; she had no idea who, or how badly, but it had clearly left deep emotional scars on Dominic. She took his hand. 'Do you want to talk about it?'

'No,' he said, and sighed. 'But I will, because I need to be fair with you. Just so you know what you're getting into. And I'll understand if you change your mind about coming to Amberhurst and you don't want to see me any more outside work—or even work with me.'

She frowned. 'Whatever it is, it can't possibly be that bad.' She was absolutely sure of that. The man she'd grown to know better was a good man. 'And I happen to like working with you. You're clear on your instructions, you treat the patients and staff with respect, and your mind works the same way that mine does.'

He took a deep breath. 'The accident was just over two years ago. Oliver—my elder brother—is now in a wheelchair. And it was my fault.'

She didn't understand how that could be, but she realised that he needed to tell her what had happened in his own time and his own way, so she remained silent.

'I wanted to beat him. We'd had this sibling

rivalry thing going for years—he'd do something, and I'd try to better it. Though not in a
nasty way,' he added swiftly. 'It wasn't putting
each other down. I guess we pushed each other
to be the best we could be. Being four years older
than me, Oliver was always the trailblazer, but I
was determined I wasn't going to be left behind;
and, the better I did, he harder he blazed the trail
because it spurred him on to be even better. I
did think about becoming a vet, specialising in
horses, but listening to him talk about his course
when he was a student decided me: I wanted to
help people, too, the way my brother did. That's
why I became a doctor.'

'Was he an emergency specialist, too?'

'No, he was a cardiac surgeon,' Dominic explained. 'I thought about specialising in surgery,
but when I did my pre-reg training I found that
I liked the rush of the emergency department. I
talked it over with Oliver, and he said that I'd be
an excellent surgeon, but he thought the variety
of the emergency department would suit me a
lot better. And he was right. I love what I do.' He
sighed. 'But this rivalry thing—it meant we had
to be as good as each other outside work, too.

Oliver used to play rugby. He was an Oxford Blue, and he could've made a career out of it, but he wanted to be a surgeon. So he used to play for a Sunday side, and coach the kids on Saturdays.' He dragged in a breath. 'For me, it was horses. I used to ride, do a bit of competition jumping and eventing, but then some of my friends joined this re-enactment group and dragged me along to see the jousting.' He smiled wryly. 'When I was Tyler's age, I was just like him. Crazy about horses, used to pretend I was a knight. I used to dress up with a bucket on my head and carry a mop around.'

She could just imagine it. He would've looked adorable.

'Then, at the re-enactment event, I discovered I'd never really grown out of it. When I got the chance to try jousting for myself…I loved it. I dragged Oliver along, and he couldn't resist it, either. He found a club in London and trained there. It's a buzz like nothing else. Speed, precision, and a special bond with your horse.'

'And yet you gave it up.' She was having real trouble understanding that. The way he talked about it made her think he'd loved the sport almost as much as he loved his job. 'Why?'

'It was the least I could do,' he said.

'How do you work that one out?'

'Oliver lost a lot more than I did.'

'What happened?' she asked softly.

'I unhorsed him in a joust.' He sighed. 'I knew I was better at jousting than he was—I'd done it for a few months longer than he had, and I'd kept up with my riding when he'd switched to rugby at university. And I knew it was risky for him—the most common injuries in a joust are broken fingers, which isn't exactly conducive to performing surgery. I should've been more careful.'

'But he knew that risk and it was his choice to accept it,' Louisa pointed out, tightening her fingers round his.

'It was my fault,' Dominic repeated.

'If someone's lance hits you, does it automatically mean you fall off the horse?'

'No. You should be able to deflect the blow—and, if you can't, you should still be able to hold on.'

'So it couldn't have been all your fault. And if

someone comes off, does it automatically mean serious injury?'

'The armour should protect you, and there's padding underneath to minimise the bruising. But, in Oliver's case, it wasn't enough.' Dominic closed his eyes. 'I can see it even now, in slow motion. Just like it felt at the time—as if everything was happening underwater, every movement so much slower than usual. Oliver falling backwards off the horse, landing awkwardly—and I couldn't get to him in time to stop it happening. I was frantic, but the faster I tried to get to him the more everything seemed to slow down.'

Just like when a child took those first faltering steps and then toppled over and banged his head; she'd heard parents say that so many times in the emergency department. And she'd lived through it herself, with Tyler. She rubbed the back of Dominic's hand with the pad of her thumb, trying to tell him without words that she understood.

He opened his eyes again. 'The emergency services were there straight away, and they put him on a board—but they couldn't do anything about the damage. The surgeon told us that Oliver had an incomplete lower spinal injury. And that was the end of everything. You can't exactly open a ribcage and perform intricate surgery on a heart if you can't stand for more than a couple of minutes at a time.' He shook his head. 'I took so much away from my brother. And he's been in pain every single day for the last two years, because of me. I have to live with that knowledge.'

'I don't know what to say.' She moved closer and wrapped her arms round him. 'Except it's taken you a lot of courage to tell me this.'

'Courage?' He gave a mirthless laugh.

'It was an accident,' she said. 'It wasn't as if you set out to hurt him on purpose.'

'The end result's the same. I wrecked his life.'

'Has he told you that?'

'He doesn't have to. Before the accident, he was a brilliant surgeon and a brilliant rugby-player—and a pretty good horseman. Now he's stuck in a wheelchair. No career, no sports, nothing.'

Louisa racked her brains to remember what she knew about spinal injuries. 'If it's an incomplete injury, there's a chance he might be able to walk again.'

'At the moment, he can only take a few steps—and they hurt like hell. He's putting himself

through an incredibly punishing physio programme. He's determined that he's going to walk
again and drive again—he's having a car spe-
cially adapted.' Dominic's face tightened. 'But
for the time being he has to rely on other people
to haul him around. And he hates it. In the early
days, he told me he wished he'd broken his neck
and died, so he didn't have to struggle through
all the pain...' His voice cracked.

She held him more tightly. 'It sounds to me as
if he was angry and frustrated and lashed out at
you because you're close to him—you're a safe
person to yell at because you understand what
makes him tick.'

'Maybe.'

'It's how you would be, too. And so would I,' she
said softly. 'It takes two to joust, Dominic. And
maybe Oliver had something on his mind, something that stopped him paying proper attention.'

'He was going to ask his girlfriend to marry
him, that evening. He'd been carrying the ring
about with him for a week.'

He didn't have to say any more; she could guess
the rest. Oliver's girlfriend hadn't been able to
cope with his disability, so the relationship had

broken up: and Dominic blamed himself for that, too. 'If his mind wasn't on what he was doing,' she said, 'then he was just as much to blame as you, if not more so.'

But Dominic's expression told her that he didn't believe it.

He was even more damaged than she was, she thought. She didn't believe enough in other people, but Dominic had it harder, because he'd lost his belief in himself. And no amount of talking from other people was going to change his mind on that score. This was something he had to come to terms with himself.

Instead, she said quietly, 'Do other people at the hospital know?'

He shook his head. 'They know my brother had a bad accident, and I've taken life a lot more seriously since then, but they don't know the details.'

'Thank you for trusting me with something so personal. And I can assure you that I'm not going to be talking about it to anyone.'

'I appreciate that.' His voice was clipped; and she just knew that he was bottling up his feelings again.

'Does Oliver know you're going to joust again?' she asked softly.

'I talked to him about it, the other night. To see how he'd feel about it. If he'd mind.'

'And?'

'He said I was an idiot, and it was about time I stopped boring my poor horse with mindless hacking.'

'Hacking?' She looked at him, mystified. 'Isn't that something to do with computers?'

He smiled, and held her closer. 'No. It's exercising a horse out on bridle paths and in the country, rather than in a schooling arena. General riding, not training for jumping, etcetera.'

'Right.' She paused. 'So when are you going to ask Ty?'

'You're still happy for him to do it, even though I told you what happened with Oliver?'

'I think you're going to be completely paranoid about safety,' Louisa said, 'so he's going to be absolutely fine.' She brushed her mouth against his. 'Come to dinner tonight. Ask him then.'

There was a look of wonder on his face. 'Seriously?'

'Did you really think I'd want nothing to do with you, once you'd told me?'

'Well—yes,' he admitted.

She stroked his face. 'It was an *accident*, Dominic. Did you go out deliberately to push your brother off his horse and break his back?'

'Of course not.'

'Well, then. I know you're blaming yourself, and I kind of understand why, but sometimes these things just happen.' She stole another kiss. 'If it had been the other way round, would you have blamed him?'

'No.'

'And would you have expected him to give up jousting and doing things he loved, just because you couldn't do them any more?'

Dominic grimaced. 'I suppose not. I know what you're saying, Louisa, but…' He shook his head. 'Every time I see the pain in his eyes that he's trying to hide from everyone else, something shreds me up inside. If only I hadn't been so keen to score points that day and make him admit that I was better than him at something. If only I'd just let it go.' He looked bleak. 'I just wish I could turn the clock back.'

'You can't,' she said. 'All you can do is learn from the past and move on. And maybe be a bit less hard on yourself.'

That, Dominic thought, was a lot easier said than done. But his spirits felt lighter after he'd talked to Louisa—sheer relief that she didn't think any less of him, now he'd told her the truth—and he duly turned up to dinner that evening. 'I need a favour from you,' he told Tyler. 'I asked your mum, and she says it's OK to ask you. I need a page.'

Tyler frowned. 'Why?'

'Because I'm jousting at Amberhurst. And someone has to hold my standard while I'm at the tilts. So I wondered if you'd like to do that. Be my page.'

'A real knight's page?' At Dominic's nod, Tyler let out a whoop of delight—and actually hugged him.

Dominic couldn't help hugging the little boy back. And when he glanced at Louisa, he could see her blinking back tears.

While Louisa finished preparing the meal, Tyler grilled Dominic on the exact duties of a page, and looked even more thrilled at the idea that he'd have to dress up accordingly. 'Your riding boots will do fine for footwear, but I'll get you leggings, a shirt and a tabard. If your mum gives me your measurements, I'll get it all arranged,' Dominic promised. Sensing that Louisa was about to offer to pay for the outfit, he added, 'It's a knight's duty to pay for the outfit of his page—and, in this case, a pleasure as well, because you're doing me a huge favour. Otherwise I'd have to ask Andy to be my page *and* my squire, and he's already going to be busy enough sorting out my harness.'

'I promise I'll do a good job,' Tyler said solemnly.

'There's also a bit in the show where I have to ride past the crowd and ask a lady for a favour,' Dominic added. 'So can I ask you, Louisa?'

'A knight's supposed to ask the woman he's in love with for her favour,' Tyler said.

Dominic and Louisa both froze.

'But I expect you'll ask Mum because I'm going to be your page and you don't want her to feel left out,' he added.

Later that evening, when Tyler had gone to bed, Dominic kissed Louisa goodbye. 'I'm sorry about earlier. For a moment, I thought he'd guessed about us.'

'No. He was trying to put himself in my shoes. I think that all that social skills training he's doing at school and my back-up at home is starting to pay off,' she said lightly.

'Probably.' Dominic paused. 'How do you think he'd feel? About you and me seeing each other, I mean?'

'It's still early days,' she said softly. 'Let's wait awhile before we tell him.'

He nodded. 'You're right. Best to take it slowly.' But right now his heart felt fuller and lighter than it had in years—and he knew it was thanks to her. Her warmth, her selflessness, that air of calm. Maybe, just maybe, she'd help him to forgive himself. And maybe, just maybe, he could do something for her, too. Repair some of the damage that Jack had inflicted when he'd rejected her and their son.

CHAPTER SIX

AT LAST the day of the jousting dawned. Tyler was up at the crack of dawn, dressed in his page's outfit. 'My tabard's the same colour as Pegasus's caparison,' he told his mother proudly. 'And, look, it's got Dominic's silver unicorn on it, to show I'm part of his team.'

Louisa ruffled his hair. 'You look wonderful. Come on, we'll get you some breakfast.'

'I'm not hungry.'

Meaning that he was too excited to eat. 'Toast,' Louisa said firmly, hiding a smile. 'Or you'll feel all light-headed later—and you'd hate to drop Dominic's standard because you were feeling all wobbly, wouldn't you?'

Tyler sat down at the dining-room table. 'He's not Dominic when he's jousting, he's Sir Hugo. That's such a cool name. I'm still thinking about what mine's going to be.'

The little boy chattered nineteen to the dozen

until Dominic collected them, and he continued to chatter all the way to Amberhurst Castle. 'Wow, Mum, look, it's a proper castle with turrets and battlements and everything!' He was almost beside himself with excitement.

The grounds of Amberhurst Castle were already crowded, with re-enactors wandering around in medieval garb and tourists milling about, eager to see the jousting.

'You can be let off page duties for a while, if you want to go and explore,' Dominic told Tyler. 'I need to go and see Pegasus, settle him down a bit.'

'Can I still wear my outfit?'

Dominic ruffled his hair. 'You bet.'

'What time do you need us back?' Louisa asked.

'The first joust is at eleven—so, maybe a quarter to?'

'Fine.' She took his hand and squeezed it. 'You OK?' she asked softly.

He took a deep breath. 'I think so. And nerves are good. It means you're not taking anything for granted and are less likely to make mistakes.'

She knew exactly what mistake he was thinking

about. 'You'll be fine. And we'll be cheering for you.'

He lifted the end of her scarf. 'Better than that, you'll be letting me wear this, for luck.'

But the smile didn't quite reach his eyes. He was really nervous, she realised. Hearing that Tyler was busy scrambling out of the back of the car, she leaned forward and brushed her mouth briefly against his. 'That's for luck.'

'No better favour could a knight ask of his lady,' he said softly. 'And you *are* my lady, Louisa.'

Desire licked all the way down her spine, and she couldn't help a breathy little sigh. 'Yes.'

'Later,' he whispered, and she nodded. Her parents were meeting her on the field later, not wanting to miss their grandson's performance as a page; she'd ask them if Tyler could have a sleepover at theirs tonight. Because, once the adrenalin had stopped flowing, she had a feeling that all the guilt would come straight back and Dominic would really need her to hold him and soothe his soul.

Dominic checked his horse over, then checked all the buckles on his armour.

'And how many times have you done that this morning, little brother?' a voice asked behind him.

He whirled round. 'Oliver!'

'It's "my lord", to you. Tsk. Knights these days really have no manners.' His brother, dressed in medieval garb and wearing a crown, grinned broadly. 'Well, Sir Hugo. It's good to see you back. You OK?'

'Yes.'

Oliver arched one eyebrow.

'All right. I'm not,' Dominic admitted. 'I keep thinking about the last time I jousted.' And the guilt was almost paralysing.

'Listen. What happened—we can't change it. And, yes, of course I'd rather be out there jousting against you today instead of being stuck in this…' Oliver indicated his wheelchair '…but it's not going to happen and it's pointless either of us droning on about it. So you're going to get on Pegasus and you're going to joust as brilliantly as you always did and you're going to come first. Got it?'

Dominic wasn't so sure. 'I've been out of the field for a while.'

'Two years, three months and nine days,' Oliver said, 'if you're going to be boring about it.'

They both knew the exact number of days. Hours, even. 'In your shoes, I'd still be raging,' Dominic said.

'Done that, and it hasn't changed anything. Time to try something else and see if that works better. And it's time you stopped obsessing over it and moved on, too.' Oliver shrugged. 'So who's the young page next to Andy?'

'Tyler. The son of a friend.'

'Friend, hmm? When do we get to meet her?'

'I didn't say my friend was female.'

'You didn't have to. It showed on your face.' Oliver regarded his brother seriously. 'Does she know about the accident?'

'Yes.'

'And she's still around. Good. You picked someone sensible. So when do we get to meet her?' Oliver repeated.

'When I'm ready. Don't be bossy.'

Oliver laughed. 'Big brother's privilege. Go out there and win for me.' He patted Dominic's arm. 'And I meant it. It's good to see Sir Hugo back. I've missed him.'

'So have I,' Dominic admitted.

'I'd better get back to the dais and do my lord of the manor bit. See you later. And I meant it about meeting your friend, too. And the page. He looks a nice kid.'

'Yes. He is.'

And then it was time to finish getting ready. Dominic made a fuss of his horse, scratching him behind the ears. 'Looking forward to this, boy?' he asked. 'And are we going to come out on top?'

The Percheron whickered and nudged him, as if to say yes.

Dominic grinned, and checked the saddle for the last time before Andy checked the straps of his armour.

He'd almost forgotten how much he loved this. There was no headier buzz than this: climbing on to the mounting block, getting astride his horse, and knowing that the joust was about to start. For the next few minutes he wouldn't be Dr Dominic Hurst: he'd be Sir Hugo de Amberhurst. He'd borrowed his stage-riding name from his Tudor great-whatever grandfather, whose portrait hung in the family gallery and whom everyone said Dominic resembled, right from when he'd been a toddler. Sir Hugo had been a legendary jouster, too, and Oliver had always teased him about being a throwback.

Automatically Dominic looked up at the dais opposite the jousting field. Oliver was sitting there, dressed in the costume of the lord of the manor, casually chatting to the people at the dais with him. The way they'd set it up, nobody who saw him would guess that the 'lord of the manor' was sitting in a wheelchair rather than on a throne.

Almost as if Oliver sensed Dominic's glance, he looked over, and raised his hand in a salute. A blessing. Wishing him well.

Dominic knew he didn't deserve it, but it warmed him.

'Ready, Sir Hugo?' Andy asked.

'Yes.'

'Good. Tyler—are you ready with the standard?'

'Oh, yes.' The little boy beamed and lifted up the banner.

'Come on, then, team,' Dominic said. 'Let's do it.'

Andy and Tyler walked out to the jousting

arena. 'Introducing the one, the only Sir Hugo de Amberhurst and his horse Pegasus!' Andy called.

Dominic heard the cheers and clapping. 'On with the show, boy,' he said softly to Pegasus, and urged the horse into a fast walk.

Louisa, who had been taking photographs of Tyler while her father was in charge of the video camera, paused as Dominic rode out. She'd seen the photographs of him in his armour, but nothing had prepared her for how incredibly sexy he looked. The black knight on a white horse, carrying a dark red shield with a silver unicorn. No wonder most of the women in the audience had dreamy looks on their faces; and she had a feeling that she did, too.

'And the one, the only Sir Simon de Leigh and his horse Midnight!' The other knight's squire waved a gold-coloured banner with a blue boar on it; moments later, Sir Simon rode out on a black horse.

Both knights did a circuit of the arena in front of the crowd; and then Dominic reined back right in front of Louisa.

He reminded her of the knight in one of the posters in Tyler's collection—Waterhouse's *Lamia*, where the knight was looking down at the kneeling woman. And, lord, he was sexy. His beautiful mouth. The hot expression in his eyes as he looked at her.

And she wanted him.

Badly.

'May I wear your favour, my lady?' he asked.

It felt as if he were claiming her in front of the whole world, and she was aware of envious glances and murmuring from other women in the crowd. 'Yes, my lord.' She stood up, removed the scarf from her neck and handed it to him. It was a pretty one, lightly woven strands of copper and gold and russet with a fringe.

'Thank you, my lady.' He smiled and blew her a kiss, and she could feel the colour flooding into her face. Then he tucked the scarf in to his helmet; it glittered against the black metal, and the fringe fluttered in the slight breeze. He gave her another smile, and her heart fluttered as much as the scarf.

Sir Hugo and Sir Simon touched their right hands together in a show of friendship and a fair fight before riding to their respective ends of the arena.

The squires gave each of the knights a lance; they held it in their right hands, pointed upwards and slightly back. At a signal, they started to canter towards each other, lowering their lances as the horses picked up speed. Louisa was surprised at how fast it was—a matter of mere seconds before she heard a shredding sound and saw the ends of the lances bursting into splinters. All the while, her heart was in her mouth. Please, God, let Dominic be safe. Let him be able to concentrate and put the past out of his mind. Please let him be all right. Please don't let him be hurt.

'That's a strike on the breastplate for Sir Simon, three points,' the commentator said. 'And a strike on the shield for Sir Hugo, five points.'

The knights did two more passes, then at the end handed their shattered lances to their squires and rode slowly along the tilting rail so they could clasp their right hands very briefly.

'There's going to be a break between the bouts, so our knights are going to remove some of their armour now and give you a chance to meet the team,' the commentator said.

Tyler was proudly holding the standard by Dominic's side; Louisa took more photographs of him, then one of Dominic. The look in his eyes made a shiver of pure desire run the whole length of her spine.

'You've got people queuing up to talk to you, so I'll see you later,' she said, and ruffled Tyler's hair. 'You did a brilliant job, darling.'

'I'm still on duty, Mum. You're not supposed to ruffle my hair,' he said, looking pained, and she couldn't help smiling.

When the meet-and-greet had finished, Dominic was able to shed his armour and join them for a wander around the castle grounds. He still looked like a medieval knight, wearing dark breeches, dark boots, an open-necked white shirt with billowing sleeves and a dark red velvet cloak.

Utterly gorgeous.

And all hers.

'This is the best day of my whole life,' Tyler said.

It was one of the best in hers, too.

Somehow Dominic ended up holding Louisa's hand as they wandered through the encampment. It felt so right, she thought. His bare skin against hers.

A shiver ran down her spine. Ty had had a wonderful day and was spending the night with his grandparents. So for once maybe she could stop worrying, let go, and just enjoy herself. Maybe tonight she could snatch one night of pure pleasure with a gorgeous, caring, attentive man. A man she found incredibly attractive, and she knew that it was mutual—the way he kissed her had become more intense over the last few weeks, and they'd both found it harder and harder to stop at just kissing.

Tonight, maybe they could take time out for *them*.

'Ty's staying at Mum and Dad's tonight,' she said softly. 'So I was wondering if you were busy.'

Dominic's eyes went wide, and he stooped to whisper in her ear, 'Do you mean…you're asking me to stay over?'

'Yes.'

He sucked in a breath. 'If you're sure—then, yes. Oh, *yes*.' His face was filled with the same wild, crazy joy that was bubbling through her entire body.

Tonight… She could hardly wait. Tonight, she and Dominic would explore each other properly. Thoroughly. And tomorrow she'd wake up in his arms. Sated. Warm. Happy.

The whole day sparkled. There was a second bout of jousting, and even though Louisa was secretly terrified by the speed and the potential for disaster as the horses galloped down the tilting rail, she knew how skilled the riders were and she enjoyed watching Dominic on Pegasus.

When the results were announced, Sir Hugo was at the top of the list—and he won the cup. She could see that Tyler was almost beside himself with joy when Dominic lifted him onto Pegasus and got him to sit there, holding the cup, while the photographs were taken. And then he beckoned to her. 'Come on. You have to be here, too. It was wearing your favour that made me win.'

'Go,' Gillian said, giving her a little push. 'And give me your camera.'

They stood either side of Pegasus, holding hands over the horse's neck, while Tyler beamed from his position on the saddle. How easily Dominic had made room in his life for Tyler. He thought about what would make the little boy happy: and yet Tyler's biological father hadn't been able to do that.

Dared she let Dominic further into their lives? Or should she still keep this just between the two of them?

Right at that moment, she wasn't sure. But one thing she knew for definite. Tonight she wanted to fall asleep in Dominic's arms. Be close to him. And, when she glanced across at him, she could see in his eyes that he was thinking along exactly the same lines.

'This is the best day *ever*,' Tyler repeated as they walked around the stalls again afterwards.

'They're doing pony rides round the lower part of the grounds. Shall we go and see what the queue's like?' Dominic asked.

'Can we?'

'Sure.' He gave the little boy a hug. 'My treat, because you were the most brilliant page.'

'When are you jousting again?'

'When the season opens, next year—the ground needs to be dry enough and soft enough so the horses don't slip,' Dominic explained. 'But, if it's all right with your mum and you want to do it, you can be my page next season. Andy can start teaching you how to check the armour, too.'

Tyler visibly swelled with pride. 'I'd love that. Can I, Mum? Please?'

How could she resist? 'Sure.'

The queue for the pony rides wasn't too bad. They waited in line, then watched as Tyler was led round the field on the pony.

Louisa wasn't sure how it happened, but suddenly the pony was rearing and Tyler was falling off in a wide arc. Even as she started running, she knew it was too late, that she'd never get there in time to catch him. With horror, she saw that his hard hat wasn't on properly either—that it was falling at a slightly faster rate than he was. Dominic, too, was running—but even his longer legs and bigger muscles weren't enough to save the little boy.

It must've been only seconds, but it felt like eternity between the moment that Tyler hit the floor and she was on her knees beside him. 'Tyler!'

'Move the pony and keep everyone back,' Dominic directed the horrified stable girl who'd been leading the pony round the field. He pulled his phone from his pocket and Louisa was aware of him talking to the emergency services controller, but most of her attention was fixed on her son.

'Tyler, can you hear me?'

There was no answer; he lay there motionless. Unconscious.

All the worst-case scenarios flew through Louisa's mind. A broken neck, spinal injury, severe brain injury…

They couldn't move him, just in case they made things worse, but she desperately wanted her son in her arms. The child she'd nursed, that she'd loved from the very first second he'd been put in her arms, wet and slippery and warm. Her baby.

'Tyler. Wake up!' Her breath came out as sobs.

Dominic was checking him over carefully, without moving him. 'His ABCs are fine.'

'He's *unconscious*, Dominic!' she snapped.

'I know, honey. And the ambulance is on its way. Try not to pan—'

'How the hell can I not panic? That's my *son* lying there.' She hissed the words at him, knowing that she was being unfair but too worried and angry to stay calm.

Supposing Tyler died? She'd spent her time thinking of the man by her side, planning to make love with him this evening, instead of looking after her child. She'd been reckless with her baby, not paying attention, letting herself get swept away by her growing feelings for Dominic. Stupid, stupid, *stupid*. If she hadn't been so self-ish, thinking of herself instead of her son, this would never have happened.

If Tyler died, if he was seriously injured and never recovered, she'd never be able to forgive herself.

Two years, three months and nine days ago. About the same time of day, too. Back then, Dominic had been on his knees as well, checking the vital signs of someone who'd come off a horse. Someone he really cared about.

The nightmare was back again. Except it wasn't just something he could wake up from. This was real.

When the jousting had gone well, he'd been so sure that life was going to be all right again. He was wandering around the place he loved most in the world, with a bright, sweet-natured woman by his side, and her son—a child he'd become increasingly fond of, the more he'd got to know the boy. And now the whole lot was unravelling right before him, just as it had when Oliver had fallen awkwardly off his horse.

Tyler was hurt. How badly, Dominic wouldn't be able to assess until the boy had recovered consciousness or was in hospital. But this was all his fault. Why had he suggested the pony ride? Why hadn't he thought to double-check that Tyler's hat was on properly? But instead he'd been thinking of Louisa, remembering the look in her eyes when she'd asked him to stay over. The promise of mutual pleasure and satisfaction and joy.

How had it all disintegrated into this mess—and so fast?

Right now, Louisa's face was blank with shock. Numb.

'Tyler,' she whispered. 'Tyler. Say something. Talk to me, darling. Say something.' Her voice was cracked with pain.

'Mum.' The word was barely a murmur, but

they both heard it. 'Mum. My head hurts,' Tyler mumbled.

'All right, darling. Just lie still—there's an ambulance on its way and they'll have something to take the pain away.' Louisa wrapped her hand round his. 'Can you feel your legs?'

'Yes. They hurt, too.'

Thank God, Dominic thought. The time to really worry would be if the little boy couldn't feel anything at all. That would mean serious damage. He could still remember the look on Oliver's face, the panic in his eyes when he'd whispered, 'Dom, I can't feel my legs...'

Please, please don't let this turn out so badly.

Please let it be just simple concussion. No complications.

Please.

He checked Tyler's respirations, then took Tyler's other hand and checked his pulse. 'He's doing OK,' he murmured to Louisa. 'Where are your parents?'

'They were going to have a cup of tea in the castle café.'

No way could either of them leave Tyler to try and find them; but he could still take that worry from her shoulders. 'Give me their mobile number and I'll call them, tell them what's happened.'

Even though she was clearly frantic, her medical training stood her in good stead, because she remained calm and focused. 'My mobile's in my handbag. Use that. It's under "Mum mobile".'

He took the phone from her bag and found the number, and explained the situation rapidly to Gillian Austin. The Austins were there within minutes; as soon as he could see that Louisa had the support she needed, he withdrew slightly and called Andy.

'There's been an accident in the lower field. Tyler's hurt and an ambulance is on its way. Can you tell everyone what's happened and look after Pegasus for me? I want to go to hospital with Ty and Louisa.'

'Will do. Ring us when you know how he is,' Andy said. 'Ric or me'll come and get you.'

'Thanks, mate. I will.'

When the ambulance arrived, Dominic gave the paramedics a full run-down of what had happened and Tyler's condition. 'We're probably looking at concussion, but with that distance of fall I don't want to take any chances.'

'We'll put him on a spinal board,' the paramedic said.

Between them, they transferred the little boy to the ambulance.

'I'm coming with you,' Dominic said as Louisa climbed into the back of the ambulance.

'But you've got things to do here.'

'It's all sorted. You and Tyler are my priority,' he said, and climbed in beside her.

Louisa held Tyler's hand all the way to the hospital.

'I'm scared, Mum,' he said, his teeth chattering.

So was she. So scared that her entire body felt as if it were about to shatter into tiny shards. The back of her neck was burning with adrenalin and she could taste bile. But, for Tyler's sake, she forced herself to sound calm. 'I'm here, darling. Nothing's going to hurt you while I'm here.'

'And Dominic.'

'I'm here,' Dominic confirmed. 'I'm not going to let anything happen to the best page I've ever had.'

The journey felt as if it took seconds and days,

both at the same time. Then at last they were in the emergency department at the hospital.

'Mr and Mrs Austin, would you like to wait in the relatives' room?' the doctor asked.

'This is Dr Hurst and I'm Tyler's mother, Louisa Austin,' Louisa said, her voice clipped. 'And, no, we wouldn't like to wait in the relatives' room, thank you. I promise we won't get in your way—we both work in an emergency department so we know what it's like—but there's absolutely no *way* I'm letting my son out of my sight.'

'Very well.'

The doctor checked Tyler over, and Louisa watched his face intently, looking for signs of things he wasn't saying. Did he think it was more serious than concussion? She clenched her fists in a vain attempt to stop herself shaking. But waiting grew harder and harder, and in the end she couldn't help asking, 'Do you think there it's just concussion or are there fractures?'

'We're sending him to X-Ray now,' the doctor said. 'I'll be able to tell you more when the X-rays are back.'

'And you'll ask Radiology for AP, lateral and Townes views?' she asked.

The doctor looked slightly wary. 'Yes.'

'That's what I would've asked for, too,' Dominic said. 'There's been no blood or fluid from his nose and ears, but he was knocked out. I have a very low index of suspicion on head injuries where children and the elderly are concerned, and I guess it's the same here.'

The doctor nodded. 'Mrs Austin, this is a completely routine exam. Tyler's talking and he's making sense, so that's a very good sign.'

Louisa lowered her voice so Tyler wouldn't hear. 'For now—you know how quickly children can deteriorate.'

Dominic wrapped his arms round her. 'Louisa, I know you've got all the worst-case scenarios running through your head, but they're all rare,' he said, keeping his voice equally low. 'The chances are, it's just concussion and nothing to worry about.'

'You don't know that. Not until the X-rays are back. And I need to go with my son.'

'Of course, Mrs Austin.'

She looked at Dominic. 'Mum and Dad were following us in the car. They'll be here in a minute. Can you wait for them and tell them where I am?'

'Of course I will.'

She went to the radiology department with Tyler, reassuring him and staying within his sight behind the screen as the X-rays were taken.

By the time they got back to the emergency department, her parents were there, talking to Dominic. She waved, but stayed next to her son, holding his hand.

It felt like for ever, waiting for the X-ray results to come back, but at last the doctor came over. 'I'm glad to say everything's clear, but I'd like him kept in overnight in the children's ward for observation, because of the distance he fell. That isn't a cue for you to start worrying. I'm just being super-cautious—like your friend, I have a low index of suspicion for head injuries in children and the elderly.'

'Can I stay with him?' Louisa asked.

'Of course you can,' he said. 'I'll take you up to the ward myself and introduce you.'

'Thank you.' She blinked back the tears. 'I'm sorry I was stroppy with you earlier.'

'When it's your own child, you can't help it.

I've got a six-month-old daughter,' the doctor said sympathetically. 'And my wife says I'm a nightmare—if Zoe gets the slightest sniffle, I'm checking her temperature and her breathing and thinking of all the differential diagnoses. The really scary ones.'

'Tell me about it,' Louisa said ruefully.

Once they were settled on the ward and Tyler had fallen asleep, Gillian said, 'We'll go and fetch some things for him—pyjamas and his wash things. And something for you to change into. I've got your spare key, love, so we'll go now and we'll be back as soon as we can.'

'Thanks, Mum.'

'And I'm staying,' Dominic said softly. 'At least until your parents get back. I'm so sorry, Louisa. If I hadn't suggested the pony ride, this wouldn't have happened.'

She swallowed hard. 'It wasn't your fault the pony reared.'

'No, but it shouldn't have happened. And why didn't someone check his hat?' He shook his head. 'I should've done that myself.'

'I thought Ty knew how to do it. He always sticks by the rules.'

'But maybe he was just so excited, he forgot. Again, that's my fault. If I hadn't asked him to be my page, he would've been just a spectator. He would still have been excited, but he wouldn't have been sidetracked.' He shook his head. 'I'm so sorry.'

Louisa bit her lip. 'He's so precious to me. If anything happens to him…' The idea was so shocking that she couldn't breathe.

Dominic wrapped his arms round her. 'I'm sure it's simple concussion. I checked those X-rays myself, just in case anything had been accidentally missed, and everything looked fine. The doctor was just being very cautious and that's how I would've handled this, too—and it's how you would've expected it to be handled if the patient was a stranger instead of your son.'

She knew that was true, but she couldn't push the fear away. 'If something happens to him…'

'It won't.' He held her close. 'Of course you're worried. You're his mother and he means the world to you.' He paused. 'He means a lot to me, too. I wanted him to have the most fantastic day today, to make some really good memories—and I'm so sorry it's turned out like this.'

She felt a tear slide down her face and scrubbed it away. 'I feel so guilty. If I hadn't been thinking about tonight, about having you all to myself and...' Her breath hitched. 'This feels like payback.'

'No,' he said firmly. 'It wasn't your fault. And you and me...that'll keep. When Tyler's back on his feet.'

She said nothing, not having the strength to have a row about it, but she wasn't sure there could be a 'you and me' with Dominic. Not now. Because if she hadn't been so damn selfish and put herself first, her son wouldn't be lying here now.

And yet, at the same time, it felt so good to have someone to lean on. Someone to share the worries with. She'd spent so many years on her own, being strong; was it so wrong to lean on a shoulder when it was offered?

Torn between pushing Dominic away and sobbing on his shoulder, she took refuge in silence. Dominic sat quietly with her, just holding her, while Tyler slept. And finally Gillian arrived at the ward again.

'I brought your things, love,' she said. 'And I'll

stay with you. We can take turns keeping awake and watching over him.'

'And that's my cue to go,' Dominic said.

Louisa frowned. 'But you came with us in the ambulance. How will you get home? We're miles from Brighton.'

'Don't worry, Andy or Ric will come and pick me up. And I'll call Essie, tell her what's happened and get her to arrange cover for you. They'll probably discharge him in the morning and I assume you'll want to stay with him for a few days.'

'I...' Louisa found herself shaking uncontrollably. 'Yes.'

'If anything changes,' he said, 'I want you to promise me that you'll call me. No matter what time of night or day it is. And I'll be there straight away.'

She swallowed the threatening tears. 'Thank you.'

'Promise me.'

'I'll call you.' At the intense look on his face, she added, 'I promise.'

He wrapped his arms round her. 'Hang on in there. He's going to be fine. And I'll speak to you tomorrow, unless you need me here before then.'

Louisa and Gillian stayed at Tyler's bedside, taking turns to doze for a couple of hours while the other watched over the little boy. And, the next morning, just as Dominic had predicted, Tyler was discharged. Gillian drove them home and Louisa sat in the back with Tyler, holding his hand and thanking God that her little boy was safe. She'd never, ever put anyone before him again.

CHAPTER SEVEN

But, in the middle of the morning, Tyler was violently sick.

'Mummy, my head hurts,' he whispered.

'Worse than yesterday, or better, or the same?' she asked, trying to keep her voice as even and controlled as she could.

'Worse,' Tyler said, looking woebegone. 'It really hurts.'

It wasn't uncommon for children to be sick after a head injury, but she had a bad feeling about this. She needed him checked over—right now.

'All right, sweetheart. Let's go and get you checked over.' She called an ambulance, giving them full details of Tyler's symptoms and the background.

All the way to the hospital, holding Tyler's hand, she thought about it. Was it an extradural haemorrhage—bleeding into the space between the skull and the brain, caused by a rupture in an artery? The blood clotted and caused pressure in the skull, which in turn caused headaches, drowsiness, vomiting and seizures; it could take several days for the clot to grow and symptoms to turn up. If Tyler had a clot…

He was sick twice more in the ambulance, and the best she could do was wipe his face with a cool, damp cloth.

Please, let them get to hospital.

And let them be in time.

She'd never forgive herself if anything happened to her precious child.

Dominic was there to meet them in the ambulance bay. He took one look at her face and gave her a brief but fierce hug. 'You're in the right place, Louisa. Don't borrow trouble.'

The paramedics gave him all the information about the observations they'd taken, and Dominic examined Tyler swiftly. 'CT scan, I think,' he said.

Louisa swallowed hard. So he suspected a clot, too.

'I have a low index of suspicion with children and the elderly, remember,' he told her, clearly picking up on her worries.

It seemed to take for ever for the scan. And as soon as she saw the image on the screen, she knew. There was a definite clot.

Liam, the neurosurgeon, came straight down to see her. 'It's an extradural haemorrhage. We're going to drill burr-holes in his skull to release the clot, then we'll tie off the bleeding vessel. Try not to worry, because all the signs are good. His breathing is fine and his pupils aren't too bad, and there's no sign of any paralysis.'

But all Louisa could think about was the classic 'talk and die' scenario, where the patient appeared to get better and then collapsed.

Dominic nudged her. 'Louisa?'

She blinked, shaking her head. 'Sorry—I'm all over the place. What did you say?'

'Liam needs to know. Has he eaten anything this morning?'

'Two pieces of wholemeal toast with Marmite and no butter, and a large glass of milk—the same as he always has for breakfast. I think it all came up when he was sick.'

'That's good, because it means his stomach's empty,' Liam said. 'Now, stop worrying. He's in good hands, and you know that.'

'He's my baby,' she said, her voice a scratchy whisper.

'I'll take care of him, Louisa,' Liam promised.

She dragged in a breath. 'I need to tell Mum and Dad what's going on, but I can't leave Ty.'

'Give me their number, and I'll ring them,' Dominic said.

She took her mobile phone from her handbag and promptly dropped it because her hands were shaking so much. 'Sorry.'

He retrieved it for her. 'It's OK, honey. He's in good hands.'

'I can't stop thinking,' she whispered, 'about what could happen.'

He wrapped his arms round her. 'Go through all the muscles and all the veins and all the nerves, count backwards from a thousand in thirteens—whatever helps to fill your head and leaves no room for thoughts like that. What's your mum's number?'

'It's under "Mum home".'

'I'll call her now and I'll be up with you as soon as I can.' He rested a hand on her shoulder. 'Hang on in there. He's going to be fine. I promise.'

She swallowed the bile in her throat. 'You can't

promise that, Dominic. It's not under your control—or mine.'

'Liam's the best there is. I trust him. And that's
why I can promise,' he said softly. 'Go to Theatre.
I'll be there soon.'

She went up to Theatre with Tyler, and stayed
while they gave him a pre-med and shaved his
hair. 'You're going to be fine. I know the surgeon,' she reassured him, 'and he's brilliant. He'll
sort it out and your head will stop hurting.'

But when the anaesthetist came to give Tyler
the general anaesthetic and she was forced to
wait outside Theatre, every second felt like a
lifetime.

She was sitting with her head in her hands,
praying silently, when Dominic joined her.

'Right now you need to be held, and that's
exactly what I'm going to do—hold you.' He
wrapped his arms round her.

She was shaking. 'Dominic, if he dies...'

'He's not going to die. He's in the best hands
and your instinct was spot on. You got him here
early enough for them to do something about
it.'

How could he be sure? She wasn't. She didn't

know anything, any more. All her years of nursing training meant nothing.

Part of her wanted to push him away. She'd promised herself she'd never ever put anyone before Tyler again, and here she was, letting Dominic wrap her in his arms like he had yesterday. Leaning on him.

But she was so scared. So very, very scared. And she needed to be held. She so desperately needed someone she could lean on. Dominic was solid and reliable and *there.*

'I spoke to your mum. Your parents are on their way right now.' He gave her phone back to her.

'Thank you.' She dragged in a breath. 'I keep thinking of the cases I've seen in the past. Cases where—where they…' She couldn't get the word out. Couldn't say it in case she made it come true. *Cases where they died.*

'Every case is different,' Dominic said. 'I know it's easier said than done, but try not to think about them. Tyler isn't going to die. Liam's a brilliant surgeon and he won't let that happen.'

He was still holding her when her parents rushed into the waiting area, asking questions at a hundred miles an hour; Dominic calmed them down and reassured them, the same way he'd reassured Louisa.

'Thanks for waiting with me until Mum and Dad got here,' she said when her parents finally sat down. 'And I'm sorry for keeping you from work.'

'You're not. Essie's got someone in to cover for me. I'm staying with you at least until Ty's out of Theatre.' He stroked her hair. 'And now that's clear, I'm going to get you all a hot drink. Don't argue. It'll give you something to do and stop the wait being so bad.'

The hot drink turned out to be sweet tea. She pulled a face. 'This is horrible.'

'Yes, but you know as well as I do that it's effective, so drink it—that goes for all of you,' Dominic directed. 'And it's occurred to me, Gillian and Matt—Louisa knows what the surgical procedure is, but you don't.' He grabbed a pad and pen from his pocket and drew a swift sketch to show her parents where the clot was. 'What the surgeon's going to do is drill some holes into the skull here, take out a little lid of bone, and then remove the clot and tie off the blood vessel so it doesn't bleed again. It sounds an awful lot more scary than it is, and Tyler will be absolutely fine afterwards. He'll heal nicely.'

But the waiting dragged on and on and on.

Were there complications? Louisa wondered silently. Had something gone wrong? Was Liam going to come out of Theatre, looking drained and empty, and tell them that he'd done his best but he hadn't been able to save her son? Oh, God, no. Please don't let her lose him. He was the light of her life. Without him…

The thought was so terrifying that she couldn't breathe.

Every time she glanced at the clock, only a few seconds had dragged by. Each minute seemed like a lifetime; and each time she glanced up a little more hope seeped out of her heart. Her baby, her precious baby… How was she going to bear it without him? How could she carry on with a Tyler-shaped hole in her life?

When Dominic fetched sandwiches for them, she shook her head. 'I can't eat.' Swallowing would choke her.

'You have to eat,' he said, relentless. 'If you don't eat to keep your strength up, you're not going to be much use to Ty, are you? And he's going to need you after this.'

'What if—?' she began.

'No,' he cut in. 'Don't borrow trouble. These things take time. It feels like years out here and nanoseconds in Theatre. And it's better that Liam's thorough than if he rushes the job. It's going to be fine.'

At last, Liam and the neuro team came out.

And he was *smiling*.

Everything was all right.

Louisa closed her eyes and offered up a prayer of thanks.

'I'm delighted to tell you that the op was a success,' Liam said. 'I've removed the clot, located the bleed and tied off the blood vessel. I want him to stay in for a week, just while he's getting over the op, and then he can go home. He'll have headaches for a while, but he'll be absolutely fine. He's in the recovery room at the moment, coming round, and you should be able to see him in a few minutes.'

Her baby was safe.

Tyler was going to be all right.

All the worry and the fear stopped; and she'd

been tense for so long, holding herself together, that she simply imploded. She burst into tears, sobbing out all the worry and the nightmares; and Dominic held her, letting her cry all over him.

'It's OK,' he whispered. 'You don't have to be brave any more. I'm here. I'm not going anywhere.'

Finally, she was all cried out; when she lifted her head off his shoulder, she saw that she'd soaked his shirt.

'I'm so sorry. I didn't mean to bawl all over you.'

'It's relief,' he said softly. 'You know that—we see enough relatives being brave, holding everything in, fearing the worst; and when they know everything's all right they know they can let go and that's when they start crying. Come on, let's go and splash some water on your face, and then you can see Ty.'

The coolness of the water against her skin made her feel better, and she'd managed to pull herself together by the time the anaesthetist came out to tell her that she could go in and see her son.

'Aren't you coming?' she asked when Dominic hung back.

He shook his head. 'It's not my place. But I'll come and see him when he's settled on the ward. You know where I am if you need me.'

She could see from his eyes that he was sincere; he really would be there, if she needed him. Yet she still couldn't shake the feeling: if she hadn't got involved with Dominic and agreed to let Tyler take part in the jousting day rather than be just a spectator, this wouldn't have happened. Her attention would have been completely on her son, as it should've been, instead of partly on the man who'd tempted her to risk her heart again.

So maybe she should heed the warning and back off. At least until Tyler was old enough to look after himself more.

Which made her feel incredibly guilty about leaning on Dominic just now, letting him believe that there could be more between them—but, in future, they'd better stick to being colleagues.

Though Dominic didn't make it easy for her. He visited every morning before his shift, during every lunch break, and every evening at the end of his shift. On day three, when Tyler was starting to get bored and irritable and sick of being cooped up in bed, he produced a magnetic chess set and taught the little boy to play. 'Chess,' he said to Tyler, 'is the best game in the world. And, better still, you can play it any time. You can even play it long-distance—my brother and I used to play by email when we were students. He'd send me his move, and then I'd send him mine.' He grinned. 'Nowadays, we do it by text.'

And at the same time he nagged Louisa about eating properly, kept her in touch with what was happening on the ward, and brought in tubs of prepared out-of-season strawberries to tempt Tyler's appetite and, she suspected, her own.

Although Louisa tried psyching herself up to say to Dominic that they should stop seeing each other, she couldn't do it. Not when Tyler didn't stop talking about him. Plus she saw the way Tyler's face brightened as Dominic arrived, and the enjoyment mirrored in Dominic's eyes as they got out the chess board. How could she destroy that growing friendship and closeness? And Dominic never, ever missed a visit. He might get someone to call up and say he'd be late, but he was always, always there.

When Tyler was well enough to be discharged,

Dominic continued his visits, except at her house rather than the ward. Every morning on his way to work he dropped in to start a game of chess with Tyler, and every evening on his way to the stables he called in, made Louisa a cup of tea and handed her a magazine or book to make her sit down and take a few minutes' break, and finished off the chess game.

Though she noticed that Dominic had stopped touching her. No hugs, no hand-holding, no resting his hand on her shoulder. And, whenever he left, he kissed her cheek. Not her mouth.

So had he, too, had second thoughts about their relationship? Yet, if that were the case, surely he would've stopped visiting Tyler? Not that she could ask. She didn't have the energy: and, besides, she wasn't sure what she wanted the answer to be. She was bone-deep tired, miserable and lonely, and she couldn't see a way through it. Not without having a heart-to-heart with Dominic—a conversation that she didn't want to start.

But eventually Louisa let her mother persuade her into letting her look after Tyler during the day so she could go back to work. Gillian promised faithfully to call her if she had even the slightest worry about Tyler.

Although it felt strange to be back in the department, after two weeks off nursing her son, Louisa's first day back coincided with a cold snap and she didn't have time to think about anything except work. The waiting area was filled with people who'd slipped on the ice and put their hands out to save themselves, landed awkwardly and come to the emergency department in pain. Louisa was kept busy taking patient histories, getting them to show her with their good hand the position of their wrists when they'd fallen, and then sending them off for X-rays. Though she knew even before she sent them what the pictures would tell her: there was a classic Colles' fracture at the end of the distal radius.

For those who had fractures where the bone was in a good position for the break to heal normally, she put a backslab on and rested their arm in a sling. 'You'll need this to splint your arm for a couple of days until the swelling comes down, and then you'll see the fracture clinic to have a lightweight cast fitted,' she explained to her patients. 'You might need a second cast, a couple of weeks later, and you'll be in plaster for up to six weeks.' In two cases, the bone had moved so the patient needed anaesthesia and manipulation to get the bone back in the right place for healing. But in all cases she gave the standard advice to rest the fracture as much as possible, hold it above the heart, and make sure they didn't get the cast or backslab wet as they didn't dry out easily.

Her tenth patient of the day with a Colles' fracture was an elderly woman, and Louisa was careful to check about a history of osteoporosis.

'You know, you're the only one of my patients today who hasn't moaned about the ice,' she said as she examined Miss Castle's hand.

Miss Castle laughed. 'My dear, I've lived through far worse winters than this. Nineteen forty-seven was a terrible winter, with snow on the ground for months, and the drifts were thirty feet deep.'

'We certainly don't get snow like that nowadays,' Louisa agreed. 'That must've been hard to live with.'

Miss Castle nodded. 'Coming just after the end of the war—yes, it was tough. The power stations ran out of coal, so we had power cuts for five hours at a time. The gas pressure was so low that the light would go out and people had to be careful or they'd end up poisoned or with a huge explosion.'

Louisa thought of the last winter, and how only a few centimetres of snow had brought the country to a standstill. 'Do you remember much of it?' she asked.

'Oh, yes.' Miss Castle smiled. 'Apart from having snow feathers on the inside of the windows every morning, I remember we had to keep digging my father's car out of the snow—he was a GP. One day, it was so deep that we couldn't get the car out, so he borrowed the milkman's horse to see his patients. But the horse was used to his daily rounds and insisted on stopping and waiting at every place he normally stopped with the milkman!'

Louisa was charmed. Tyler would love that story, and so would Dominic. Maybe she'd tell them both that evening.

But then in the late afternoon Essie came in to see her, looking grim. 'I need you in Resus—there's been a bad RTA,' she said. 'A young lad's car slid on the ice and smashed into a tree. He seems fine, but the paramedics are bringing him in for a check over. The passenger, his dad, is in a bad way, though.'

'I'll come straight through.'

Dominic came in with the trolley after the handover. 'Eric Scott, aged 43. He was on the side where the car hit the tree, so he has multiple injuries—query spinal injury as well as the usual suspects from blunt trauma. No known allergies, not on any medication, and no medical conditions we need to be aware of. Not sure when he last ate, though.'

The anaesthetist was already on hand; once Eric Scott had been resuscitated, he'd be whisked up to surgery. Eric was laid flat, his neck stabilised with a rigid collar and tape.

The team swung into action to put him on oxygen, insert cannulas, get vital-signs measurements through a pulse oximeter and ECG and take blood samples. 'I want a litre of Hartmann's run in, cross-match six units, and blood samples sent for FBC, Us and Es, and glucose,' Dominic said. 'And I need someone to call Radiology and arrange X-rays—I want lateral cervical spine, chest and anterior-posterior pelvis.'

Eric was still unconscious; his blood pressure was low and his respiration rate was high. 'Looks like a thirty per cent blood loss—so I want a second litre of Hartmann's in after the first,' Dominic said.

Carefully Louisa cut through Eric's clothes to expose his chest so Dominic could examine him. 'Can you note this, Louisa?' he asked as he listened to Eric's chest. 'Sounds on both sides, might have cracked ribs but no sign of flail chest.' He glanced at the monitor. 'His blood pressure should be rising by now—he's losing blood from somewhere.'

Louisa glanced at the ECG. 'Dominic, he's in VF.' VF or ventricular fibrillation meant that electrical activity in the heart had become chaotic, so the lower pumping chambers of the heart were contracting rapidly and fluttering rather than beating. They needed to convert this back into a normal rhythm or they would lose their patient.

Dominic breathed out sharply. 'We're not going to lose you, Eric. Hang on in there.' He glanced at the team. 'Defib.'

He placed the gel pads and paddles in the correct position and checked the ECG. 'Still VF,' he confirmed. 'Charging at two hundred, stand clear—shocking now.' They waited ten seconds to see if the ECG trace changed.

'Charging to two hundred again,' Dominic said, keeping the paddles on the gel pads. 'And clear. Shocking now.'

Again, the ECG trace didn't change. 'Trying three-sixty now, Charging, clear—shocking now.'

But still there was no change. Dominic gave Eric 1 mg of adrenalin. 'CPR, Louisa, can you bag, please?'

She already had the equipment to hand. 'Five compressions, one breath?' she asked.

After a minute of CPR, they did a cycle of shocking again; there was still no response.

'I'm not going to lose you, I'm *not* going to lose you,' Dominic muttered.

They continued the cycles of CPR, adrenalin and shocking.

After twenty minutes, Louisa placed her hand on Dominic's arm. 'His brain's been without oxygen for twenty minutes. He's gone,' she said gently. 'You need to call it.'

'No. One more cycle,' he said.

But it was hopeless.

'Dominic. Call it,' Louisa said softly, 'or I will.'

She could see the muscle flicker in his cheek.

'Everyone else agreed?' he asked.

They nodded.

'Time of…' Dominic's breath hitched. 'Time of death, five thirty-two. Thank you for your help, everyone.' He swallowed hard. 'I'd better go and see the family.'

He looked drained and miserable. And he'd let her lean on him when she'd needed propping up; it was time for her to return the favour. 'I'll come with you,' she offered.

Dominic looked at her, and realised that she understood what was going through his head. That, since Oliver's accident, not being able to save a patient had always hit him harder. 'Thank you,' he said quietly. 'Just give me a second, can you?'

He lingered beside the body and put his hand on Eric Scott's shoulder. 'I'm so sorry. I did my best, and it wasn't enough. God bless,' he whispered, and dragged in a breath before joining Louisa outside the doors to Resus.

'His son's in the family room,' Louisa told him. 'Ian Scott, aged eighteen.'

'Eighteen? Poor kid.'

'He's been checked over and he's fine.'

'OK.' Dominic really, really hated this part of the job—where he took all the hope away from the relatives.

And it would be harder still for this family because there was nobody to blame, no stupid drunk-driver who'd been too arrogant and self-ish to consider the lives of others before getting behind the wheel of a car. Just an accident on the ice, which nobody could have prevented.

He walked with her in silence to the family room. Eric Scott's wife wasn't there yet but his son was pacing up and down, looking anxious. As they walked into the room, hope filled his face. 'Is Dad…?' He stopped abruptly as he saw their serious faces. 'Oh, no. Please, *no.*'

'Come and sit down, love,' Louisa said.

'I'm so sorry, Ian,' Dominic told him. 'We did everything we could, but your father had a heart attack and we couldn't get him back.'

'No, he can't—not Dad.' Ian gave a sobbing

breath. 'He can't be dead. I haven't even got a scratch. How can Dad be…?'

'That side of the car took the majority of the impact,' Dominic said gently.

'But he can't be dead. He can't be. He *can't*.'

'I'm sorry, love.' Louisa put her arm round him.

'I killed Dad,' Ian said brokenly.

'No, love, the accident killed him,' she reassured him.

'The car—I couldn't do anything. It was sliding and I couldn't brake, couldn't do anything.' He dragged in a breath. 'I wasn't driving fast, wasn't showing off. I just wanted to pick my dad up from work. It's his birthday.' The boy's face worked. 'My tutorial tomorrow morning was cancelled so I knew I could come home and surprise him, say happy birthday in person instead of phoning him. I was going to take him and Mum out to dinner tonight. He was so pleased to see me when he came out of the office. And now he's dead, and it's my fault, and… Oh, God, I wish I hadn't come home and I'd never, ever got behind the wheel of the car!' He collapsed into sobs on Louisa's shoulder.

Dominic crouched in front of Ian's chair and took the boy's hands between his. 'Listen to me, Ian. It was an accident, and it could've happened to anyone. We see lots of people in here whose car has hit a patch of black ice and they've lost control. Even really experienced drivers struggle on ice, so it's not your fault and you're *not* to blame.'

'How am I going to tell Mum?'

'I'll be here with you,' Dominic said. 'I'll help you tell her—but what you need to focus on is that your dad was unconscious, so he wasn't in any pain, and he loved you very much.'

'Do you have any brothers or sisters?' Louisa asked gently.

'No, there's just me.'

'You and your mum still have each other and you'll get through this together,' Dominic said. 'It's going to be tough and you're going to have bad days, but you'll get through this. You just have to keep remembering that this was an accident, one of those things that nobody has any control over.'

A few minutes later, Essie brought Mrs Scott in. She enveloped her son in her arms. 'Ian, the hospital called me and said you were in an accident. Thank God you're all right.' Then she took in the fact that he was sobbing, Eric wasn't there, and Dominic and Louisa weren't smiling.

'Eric?' Horror filled her face. 'No. *No.*'

'I'm sorry,' Dominic said softly. 'He never regained consciousness. We did our best to get him back but I'm sorry, we simply couldn't get his heart started again.'

While he comforted them, Louisa fetched some hot sweet tea and persuaded the Scotts to drink it—just as Dominic had made her drink the stuff after Tyler's accident, knowing that it really was the best thing for shock.

'Can I see him?' Mrs Scott asked.

'Of course you can,' Dominic said, and took her through to where Eric's body lay.

While she'd gone to sort out the tea, Louisa had asked Jess to make sure that Eric's body was covered with a blanket and his face had been washed, to make it easier for his wife and son to see him.

'Take as much time as you need,' Dominic said gently.

'I can get the hospital chaplain for you, if you like?' Louisa offered.

'No, I just want to be alone with him— Oh, Eric.' A tear rolled down Mrs Scott's face as she stroked her husband's forehead. 'How are we going to manage without you?'

'I'll be in my office if you need me,' Dominic said. 'Anything you need, just ask.' He mouthed to Louisa, 'I'm going to sort out the paperwork.'

She could see the strain in the lines around his mouth. Whether he wanted to or not, he needed to talk about this—and she was about the only person who could do this. She'd call her mum and warn her that she'd be late, stay with the Scotts for a little longer, and then she'd tackle Dominic.

CHAPTER EIGHT

DOMINIC stared at the computer screen, not seeing any of the words written there. All he could see was Ian Scott's face, the shock and horror mingling there when he'd learned that his father was dead. The way he'd blamed himself for the accident.

A feeling Dominic knew well: one he'd lived with for more than two years. He too had been in an emergency room while someone he loved had been in Resus, wired up to monitors. Thankfully Oliver had been so fit that his body had been able to cope with the trauma and his heart hadn't given out. Dominic knew he was lucky that Oliver was still alive, but he also knew that his brother, despite the brave face he put on it, was in pain every single day—and it had taken months of hard work to get him to the point where he was now.

He was still brooding when there was a knock on his door. He lifted his head. 'Louisa.'

'Don't say a word. Just drink it.' She handed him a mug.

He took a sip of what he discovered was disgustingly sweet tea, and gagged. 'Thank you for the thought, but this is—'

'Disgusting, I know, but shut up and drink it,' she cut in. 'Essie just told me you almost never lose a patient in Resus and you take it twice as hard as everyone else. She doesn't know why, but I think I do, so just drink it.'

It was drink it or talk—so, despite the fact that he loathed the stuff, he drank the hot, sweet tea.

'It's brought everything back to you, hasn't it?' she asked gently. 'Being in Resus with your brother.'

There was no point in lying. 'Yes.'

'We see lots of people in here whose car has hit a patch of black ice and they've lost control. Even really experienced drivers struggle on ice.' She paused. 'So you don't blame Ian for the accident.'

'No, of course not. He's just a kid. He hadn't even been driving that long.'

'Can you hear yourself?' she asked softly. 'You

could be talking about yourself. What happened with Oliver was an accident, too.'

'An accident that should never have happened. That wouldn't have happened if I hadn't been trying to prove a point.'

'But you don't know that, Dominic. Jousting's dangerous. It could've happened anyway.' She shook her head. 'It's time you let go and stopped trying to be perfect.'

Perfect? She had to be kidding. He knew he was very, very far from perfect.

'You're human. Are you going to beat yourself up for losing Mr Scott—even though he had multiple injuries and the senior consultant wouldn't have been able to save him either?'

'I hardly ever lose a patient.'

'I know you go above and beyond, Dominic. And I know why you do it—you're still trying to make up for what happened with your brother. But you're going to have to come to terms with the fact that nothing you do will ever be able to change the past. All you can do is move on and make the future a better one. You're still crucifying yourself—and it's hurting those who love you as well as hurting you. It's time you moved on.'

Her words hit him on the raw, and he couldn't help lashing out. 'You're a fine one to talk.'

'What do you mean?'

'The way you've been, this last couple of weeks. I know you're worried sick about Ty, so I've tried to give you some space, but you've been sticking up a brick wall between us. You're blaming yourself for the accident—you think it's your fault, and just because you asked me to stay over it's some kind of cosmic payback. That you have to decide between having your son or having a relationship.'

She didn't say a word: she just stared at him, looking stricken.

'I know your ex was a self-centred bastard who didn't deserve you or his son, but that doesn't mean that all men are going to be the same. It doesn't mean that you can't lean on me in case I let you down, because I never would. I've tried to be there for you without pushing you too hard—and that's the only reason why I haven't kissed you properly since the accident—but you're not going to let me close again, are you?' He shook his head, suddenly really angry. 'You've decided you know what's best for everyone. And you're not going to give anyone the chance to have a say in it, are you? You're playing God with everyone's emotions—Tyler's and mine as well as your own—and it's not fair.'

Her face went white. She didn't say a word, just walked out.

And what made it worse was that she didn't slam the door; she closed it quietly.

The anger within him died as fast as it had risen, and Dominic raked a hand through his hair. Hell, he'd really hurt her. He hadn't meant to do that; he'd just lashed out because she'd caught him on the raw. And, although what he'd said to her was true, he could've found a more tactful way of saying it.

He needed to apologise. Now.

Quickly, he logged off the computer and went to find her, but she'd already left.

He called her mobile phone, and a recorded voice informed him that her phone was switched off.

Which meant she was probably driving; and he knew exactly where she was going. Home to her little boy.

He rang the stables. 'Ric, I'm not going to make

it tonight. Can Andy exercise Pegasus for me, please?'

'Sure. Is something wrong? Anything I can do?'

'Work,' Dominic lied. Something *was* wrong, but his best friend wouldn't be able to help with this one. This was something he needed to do himself. And he had no idea whether Louisa would even talk to him tonight, let alone open her heart and be honest with him—but he had to try.

It was too late for a florist to be open, so he went to supermarket and bought an armful of the nicest flowers he could find and then to the stationery superstore nearby and bought pencils and a sketchpad for Tyler. When he parked on the road near Louisa's house, he couldn't see her mother's car, so it meant that Gillian had gone home. Good. He liked Louisa's parents—a lot—but what he had to say was for Louisa's ears only.

He rang the doorbell and waited. Finally, she opened the door, and frowned when she saw him. 'What are you doing here?'

'Several things. You know I promised Tyler I'd

call in and see him every day to play chess with him, and I don't break my promises.' He handed her the flowers. 'And these are for you. An apology. I lashed out at you in the office and it wasn't fair of me. What you said…you were right. I'm trying to be perfect and I'm trying to make up for what I did to Oliver—and I can't do either.'

She looked wary. 'I didn't mean to be quite so harsh with you. And I'm sorry for walking out.'

'I think it's time we talked,' he said softly. 'Properly. And we need to be honest with each other.'

'Have you eaten?'

He shrugged. 'I'm not hungry.'

'Mum made a huge batch of chilli. It's in the fridge; I can heat some through for you.'

'No, you're fine.' He paused. 'Can I see Tyler now, before he goes to sleep—and then we'll talk?'

'OK.'

To his relief, she let him in. He spent a while playing chess with Tyler, talking to him about horses and admiring the pictures he'd drawn that day. And Tyler was delighted when Dominic gave him the sketchbook and pencils. 'I'll draw you on Pegasus.'

'I'd really like that,' Dominic said, meaning it.

'When I'm better, can we go swimming again?' Tyler asked.

'Sure we can.' Dominic smiled at him.

'And can I go back to the stables?'

A good question: and one he knew Louisa had been avoiding. He couldn't make the decision for her: it simply wasn't his place. 'You need to ask your mum that, not me,' he said gently. He stroked the fuzz of Tyler's hair, which had been shaved for the operation and was now starting to grow back. 'Time to get some rest, sweetheart. I'll send your mum up to give you a kiss goodnight.'

'Goodnight, Dominic.' Tyler hugged him. 'Love you.'

All the air whooshed out of Dominic's lungs. He couldn't say a word; he just hugged the little boy tightly back.

This was what it felt like to be a father.

He'd had no idea. No idea at all. It wasn't something he'd ever thought about, either before the accident, when he'd dated a string of gorgeous women, or afterwards, when he'd been too racked with guilt to think about anything else.

But now he knew. And it blew him away. This was something bigger than he'd ever felt in his life. That special feeling of knowing that you'd tackle any hurdle to make the child's life easier, no matter what it took; that you wanted to see him grow up into a man you'd be proud to call your friend. A fierce kind of protectiveness, mingled with fear and awe and wonder.

And then it really hit him.

He'd lay down his life for Tyler and Louisa.

And he wanted to be a family with them.

He wanted to be there for a whole string of firsts—Ty's first day at senior school, his first girlfriend, the day his exam results came through, his first driving lesson. All of it, the good and the bad—and even the tough times wouldn't be so tough because they'd be a family and they'd be there for each other.

Though whether Louisa would believe in him enough to let him do that was a whole different issue.

'Love you, too,' he said when he could finally speak again. 'Sleep tight.'

He found Louisa in the kitchen. 'Tyler's about to go to sleep—I said I'd send you up to give him a kiss goodnight.'

'OK. I'll go up now.'

Her eyes were huge with worry. About her son? Or about what he wanted to talk to her about? He cupped her face in his hands—and how good it felt to have her skin against his again. 'You're panicking,' he said softly. 'Don't. I'm not going to rant and rave. But we do need to talk. How about I make us both a coffee while you're tucking Tyler in?'

'Thanks. That'd be good.'

She returned to the kitchen just as he'd added milk to their coffee. 'Are you sure about the chilli?'

This wasn't just her natural hospitality, he knew. It was an avoidance tactic. 'I'm perfectly sure.' He looked at her. 'All I want to do is hold you, Louisa.'

'That's not a good idea.' She sat down at the kitchen table.

And he had a pretty good idea why: she was putting a physical barrier between them as well as a mental one. 'So I was right. You *are* backing off from me.'

'Tyler's still young. He needs stability in his life. I can't…' She shook her head and swallowed. 'This is a mess.'

'You're saying you dare not have a relationship in case it works out and he feels let down—as he was by his father?'

She closed her eyes. 'That's part of it. Which sounds so cowardly.'

'No, you're right to protect him—Tyler's only eight. He does need stability.' He paused. 'But you and I—we agreed we'd keep what's happening between us to ourselves until we knew where this was taking us. So we're no threat to his stability.' He paused. 'You said that was part of it. What's the rest?'

She dragged in a breath. 'It sounds ridiculous.'

'I can't read your mind,' he said softly. Though he had a pretty good idea what was haunting her.

'Wanting you *and* Tyler. It's greedy. Wanting it all.'

'No. It's perfectly normal. A child and a

relationship.' He took a risk. 'It's called being a family.'

She said nothing, and he couldn't read her expression at all. OK. One of them was going to have to be brave and call it. Clearly it was going to be him. 'Louisa, the accident happened. It has nothing to do with the fact that you asked me to stay over, that we were planning to make love together for the first time that night. It wasn't some kind of message to you saying that you had to give me up. It wasn't someone saying that you have to choose between us.' Had her husband given her that kind of ultimatum? Or had he simply rejected them both? Whatever, Louisa was clearly still hurting. 'You don't have to choose between me and your son. I know you come as a package. And I happen to want both parts of that package—you *and* Tyler.'

She cupped her hands round her mug. 'I don't know what to say.'

He could tell her what Tyler had said to him that evening, but he knew that would influence her decision. And he needed to know that she wanted him for himself, not just because her son had grown close to him. 'If you've decided that seeing me is a mistake because now you've got to know me better you realise you don't like me, or you don't find me attractive enough to go to bed with me, then fair enough. I won't be particularly thrilled about it—because I like you and I most definitely want to go to bed with you—but I'll accept your decision and I'll try my hardest to treat you professionally at work and be polite and friendly at the stables.' He held her gaze. 'But no other reason is good enough, Louisa. Be very clear about that.'

She dragged in a breath. 'You're pushing me, Dominic.'

'I know. And I'm going to keep pushing.' He wouldn't let her look away. 'Louisa. I like you. More than like you. And I need to know how you feel about me.'

Panic flittered across her face. 'This whole thing scares me. Before the accident, I thought I wanted to take things between us further.'

'That's what I wanted, too. So what's changed, apart from the accident?'

'I…' She shook her head in apparent frustration. 'I know what you just said, and logically I know you're right, but I can't get it out of my head. I keep thinking that it was karma. That if I hadn't wanted you so much, it wouldn't have happened.'

'That really isn't true.' He paused. 'Though I get where you're coming from. I've spent two years believing that it was my fault that Oliver had the accident, because I really wanted to prove I was better than him at something. I went over and over in my mind what happened: was the way I jousted against him any different from the way I jousted against anyone else?'

'Was it?' she asked.

'Probably not,' he admitted, 'but I don't know if I'll ever be able to get the doubt out of my head. Or the guilt.'

'And it stopped you having a relationship with anyone.'

'Before the accident, I was too busy playing and enjoying life to settle down. Afterwards...I blamed myself for what happened and I didn't feel I deserved a relationship,' he said. 'Until you. You reached me in the way nobody else could. And when you asked me to stay over that night—it was like my birthday and Christmas and every red-letter day rolled into one. I wanted you just as much as you wanted me.' He paused. 'As far as I'm concerned, nothing's changed. I still want you. But I know you've been worried sick about Ty and I didn't want to push you and make you feel that you had to split yourself between us. That's the only reason I've been holding back. Not because I changed my mind.'

'You've been very patient. Thank you.' She bit her lip. 'But I don't know where we go from here.'

'Let me make it easier for you. We'll start with a question and I want a one-word answer. Do you like me—yes or no?'

'Yes,' she whispered.

'I like you, too. I want to see you, and I think you want to see me—but you're scared that it's all going to go wrong. That you're going to get hurt. That Ty's going to get hurt.'

She nodded.

'I don't have any cast-iron guarantees,' he said softly. 'But I would never intentionally hurt you or Tyler. So that's a start. And it feels like years since I held you—and I miss you. Louisa, please?'

Just when he thought she was going to refuse, she scraped her chair back and walked round to his side of the table. He pushed his chair back, scooped her onto his lap and held her close, resting his forehead on her shoulder so he could breathe in her scent. 'Louisa. I've missed this so much.'

'I've missed it, too,' she said shakily.

He lifted his head, then looked her straight in the eye. He could see longing mixed with fear and confusion. He didn't know how to take the fear away. Or the confusion. But the longing—he could do something about that.

Slowly, gently, he touched his lips to hers. A gentle, sweet, reassuring kiss.

But once wasn't enough.

And then she was kissing him back and it was as if someone had lit touchpaper. Her hands were in his hair, his mouth was jammed over hers, and somehow his hands had slid under the hem of her top and his palms were flat against her soft, soft skin. He could feel the peaks of her nipples against his chest, and he knew that, sitting on his lap, she'd be just as aware of his own arousal.

When he broke the kiss, they were both shaking.

'I'm sorry,' he said. 'I didn't mean to come on

so strong. I…' No. If he told her exactly how he felt, he knew he'd scare her away. He had to be patient for just a little longer. Take it slowly. 'I'm sorry,' he repeated.

'It wasn't just you,' she admitted.

Hope flared. 'So this thing between us—we're still seeing where it takes us?'

'As long as Tyler comes first.'

He brushed a kiss against her mouth. 'Of course he will. And I'll try to be patient. We'll wait until he gets back on his feet before we take it further between us.' There was something else he wanted to ask her, but not yet. They needed a little time. Time for her to trust her instincts again and let him as close as he'd been before the accident. 'I'd better go now. While my good intentions still have control of me.' He moistened suddenly dry lips with the tip of his tongue. 'I want you. Very, very badly. And I think we both know it could happen right here, right now.'

Her eyes were huge. 'Yes.'

'But it's not going to. The first time between us—I want it to be special. When Tyler's staying overnight with his grandparents and neither of us is going to be worrying about him. When we have the time and space to focus on each other, just for a little while.' He stroked her face. 'I want it to be something we both remember. For the rest of our days.'

CHAPTER NINE

OVER the next couple of weeks, Tyler's condition improved and the headaches stopped, to the point where Louisa was happy for him to go back to school. And although she and Dominic were officially 'just good friends' at work and at the stables, in private they drew closer. Dominic ate with her and Tyler every night, dropping in to see them between the end of his shift and going to the stables. Tyler learned not to time him exactly, because Dominic had explained to him that the time he arrived depended on his patient; but he always rang to say he was leaving the hospital, so Louisa didn't have to guess what time to serve dinner. And she was aware of how much her son looked forward to seeing Dominic in the evenings, talking about his day and playing chess and showing him his artwork. He never stopped talking about Dominic. And she'd noticed that Tyler greeted him with the same kind of hug he reserved for her and his grandparents, and that Dominic was just as affectionate back.

Dominic also called in on his way home from the stables, for a snatched half-hour of quiet time together when Tyler was asleep. Time when they lay full length on the sofa, wrapped in each other's arms, sometimes just relaxing in each other's nearness without needing to talk, and at other times talking about their hopes and dreams. He was the first person she'd actually told that she wanted to be nursing director some day; and he'd been incredibly supportive.

'You'd make a really good job of it. Though I think you'd have to change the role so you get some hands-on time with patients. If you were stuck doing nothing but admin, you'd miss the practical side too much.' He stroked her face. 'Though you'd also get to do more teaching, and I think that'd be right up your street. And you'd be really good on the PR side.'

She felt herself go pink with pleasure. 'You really think so?'

'Really. You're fantastic with people.' He kissed her lightly. 'You're an amazing woman, Louisa Austin. And I'm proud of you.'

She'd always thought that Jack had resented her work; then again, maybe Dominic understood it more because he worked in the same area, faced the same challenges. 'Thank you,' she said softly.

'You're welcome.' He stole another kiss. 'There was something else I wanted to talk to you about. Ty's desperate to go back to his riding lessons.'

She shook her head. 'He's not ready yet.'

He raised an eyebrow. 'You mean, *you're* not ready.'

'Same thing.'

'No, it isn't. Yes, he'll probably fall off again at some point, but he learned a pretty hard lesson about double-checking your equipment. He'll never make that mistake again. Next time he comes off, he might just have a bruise, or a dent in his dignity.'

'Or a broken arm.'

'At this age, they heal quickly. And he's just as likely to get a broken arm falling over in the play-ground at school,' Dominic pointed out. 'Think how many kids his age come in to our department and end up with a backslab.'

'I'm not ready for him to go back to riding yet, Dominic.'

'Life isn't perfect and sometimes you get knocked back, but you have to get up, dust yourself down and try again.' He held her closer. 'And the thing is, he'll know that if he does fall off again, you'll be there, you'll kiss it better, and you'll help him get back on the horse again. Just as you will when he encounters other difficulties in life.'

She looked at him. 'It's not as if you went straight back to jousting after Oliver's accident.'

'That was because my head wasn't in the right place.' He sighed. 'OK, so I'm being a hypocrite.'

'And pushy.'

He refused to let her wriggle out of his arms. 'OK. But it's the Christmas party at the stables, the third Saturday in December. He'd get a huge amount from it. And it'll help him bond with the other kids.'

'You're trying to pressure me.'

'No, honey. I'm trying to help you. Yes, I admit, there is a teensy bit of riding involved—but it's all very strictly supervised, and every single rider has an assistant. They look so cute, Louisa. The kids all wear reindeer antlers on their hard hats. It's all done indoors, so there's no worry about the weather. Then, when they've had a short ride, Bea puts music on and everyone has a bit of a dance or sings along, whatever they want to do. The less mobile kids can have their faces painted if they want—then it's food, a visit from Santa, and home. They each get a present from the pony they ride—and it's just lovely.' He paused. 'Ty would really enjoy it. And so would you. And your parents would love watching him.'

'I'll think about it,' Louisa said.

He stole a kiss. 'OK. That's all I'll ask. And I won't push any more.'

'Thank you.'

'I did have another question for you.'

'Involving the stables?'

'No, but it involves you and Ty.' This was the biggie. The equivalent of asking her to go public. Would she say yes or no? 'My brother's getting married. And, um, I wondered if you'd both like to come to the wedding as my guests.'

She was silent for so long that he knew what the answer was. 'OK. Sorry for pushing. Though I could reassure you that there won't be any horses involved.'

'It's not that.' Her eyes brimmed with tears. 'It's the fact you asked Ty as well.'

'Why wouldn't I?'

'You know how direct he is. He might say the wrong thing and upset someone.'

He kissed her lightly. 'He'll be much too busy having a good time with my parents' dogs. Though I admit that'll probably mean he'll step up the nagging for a puppy afterwards.'

She frowned. 'Your parents' dogs would be at the wedding?'

'Well, not at the wedding itself.' He smiled. 'But they'll be around.'

'He'd love that.' She bit her lip. 'But I think I'd better say no. He finds a big group of people he doesn't know a bit difficult to handle. We'd probably end up leaving early and that'd put you in an awkward position.'

Dominic really didn't want to make Ty feel uncomfortable; but he had a feeling that Louisa was using her son as an excuse. Meeting his family would mean going public about their relationship, and she clearly still wasn't ready even to consider it.

He'd just have to be patient for a bit longer.

'OK.' He kissed her lightly. 'I'd better let you get some sleep. See you at work.'

But Louisa couldn't sleep that night.

Dominic had asked her to his brother's wedding. Something that would be incredibly emotional for him; he hadn't said as much, but she had the feeling that he could do with someone to lean on. Someone to help him keep the regrets and the guilt at bay.

And he'd let her lean on him. Big time. He'd pushed a little—especially where Tyler and the stables were concerned—but, when she'd said no, he hadn't shouted her down. He'd let her know his opinion, but he'd appreciated the fact that she wanted to make her own decisions.

Time, she thought, for payback. To give him a little support, the way he'd been there for her throughout Tyler's injury and his convalescence.

She called her mother the next morning, before work, to ask a favour; and, although she fully intended to find Dominic before her shift started, she discovered that he was already in Resus, dealing with a patient with a heart attack. And she was kept busy in Minors with people who'd slipped on the ice and twisted their ankles, and then a chef with a nasty burn that needed a dressing; she sent him away with notes on what to do next and a follow-up appointment to check how well it was healing. Then she was kept busy with a builder who'd slipped from some scaffolding and his ankle was swollen and painful. She took a full medical history and asked exactly what had happened when he'd fallen, so she had a better idea of how he'd landed and whether it was likely to be a bone injury or soft tissue. Although she had a feeling it was more likely to be a sprain, she sent him for an X-ray to make absolutely sure it wasn't a fracture, and checked over a teenager with a piercing that had gone septic while she was waiting for the X-ray results to come back.

A quick check on-screen showed her that there wasn't a fracture.

'That's a relief,' he said, blowing out a breath. 'I couldn't afford to be off work for weeks now, not with Christmas coming up at a rate of knots!'

'You do need to rest it for the next two days, though,' she warned him. 'The best thing you can do is prop it on a pillow so it's level with your heart, and keep it up as much as possible until the swelling goes down. If you put ice packs on— wrap in a towel so it doesn't burn your skin— that will also help with the swelling and bruising. Painkillers should take the edge off it. After a couple of days you can start to use it again, but by that I mean *gentle* exercise, to ease yourself back in. No marathons, and definitely no more using the scaffolding as a slide, OK?'

He gave a rueful laugh. 'I'll remember that!'

'I'm going to put a tubular elastic bandage on your ankle to give it support and compression, though you need to take it off before bed.' She smiled at him as she fitted the bandage. 'I know I've just rattled on at you and it's going to be hard to remember everything I said, so I'll give you a leaflet.' She quickly found the information leaflet on the computer, then printed it off.

'It's all on computer now?'

'It makes life a lot easier than finding fiddly bits of paper,' she said. 'Mind you, we always know where the sprains leaflet is. We see a lot of them in here—people who've landed awkwardly in sports, or slipped on the stairs or off a kerb. And don't start me on the evils of high heels!'

He laughed, ''Fraid I only do lace-up boots or trainers, love.'

'They'll be good support for you.' She saw him out, updated the notes and called her next patient.

How ironic that, on the day she really wanted to talk to Dominic, she didn't get a chance to have a break. She was kept busy in Minors for the rest of the day. Her last patient was a teenager who looked very sheepish and had a long, curly piece of wire sticking out of his thumb.

'I don't know if I dare ask,' she said.

'I was a bit bored in the first lesson after lunch,' he muttered. 'It's the spring from my pen. I wondered what would happen if I uncoiled it. I didn't know the end was going to be sharp.'

His mother ruffled his hair. 'You know now, love.' She rolled her eyes. 'I got a call from the school telling me he had a six-inch piece of metal sticking out of his hand, so could I please come and pick him up and I was having kittens that he'd hurt himself in metalwork! I did think about pulling it out myself, but Rob wouldn't let me. School said it was curved at the end and I should bring him here.'

'I'm such an idiot,' Rob muttered, his face turning beetroot.

'No, love, you're a teenager,' his mum said, patting his arm. 'It isn't the first time you've done something daft and it won't be the last—and your brother's the same. I'm just glad it's not a thick bit of steel stuck through your palm.'

'Does it hurt?' Louisa asked.

'A bit,' Rob admitted. 'Are you going to cut it out?'

'I'll send you down to X-Ray, and then we'll see what's there and know the best way to deal with it. Don't worry,' Louisa reassured him.

The X-ray showed that the wire was curved in slightly but wasn't too deep, so it wouldn't have to be cut out. 'I'll just snip most of it off with wire cutters,' Louisa said, 'to get it out of the way, and then I'll use forceps to take it out. It might sting a bit, but I'll be as gentle as I can.'

On the way to fetch the department's wire cutters, she bumped into Dominic. 'Hi. Busy day?'

'You're telling me.' He rolled his eyes. 'Why the wire cutters?'

'I have a teenager with a spring stuck in his hand; I need to cut most of it off to get it out of the way so that I can remove it properly.'

'Do you want me to do it? I know you're perfectly capable of doing it, but I'm a bit brawnier than you are—if the wire's thick, I can cut it more quickly than you can and that'll be less stressful for your patient.'

Typical Dominic, putting someone else first. 'Thank you. I appreciate that.' She took him through to Minors and introduced him to Rob and his mother. Dominic wielded the wire-cutters; the spring proved to be tough, and Rob gave a muttered 'Ow!'

'Sorry, Rob,' Dominic said as the spring came out.

''S OK,' Rob said. 'It's out now.'

Louisa checked the spring against the X-ray. 'Out cleanly, so you should be fine—your thumb might be a bit sore for a day or two, but you don't have to worry about infection. Let me clean that for you with a bit of antiseptic.'

Dominic chatted to Rob, keeping his mind off

the fact that his thumb was stinging as Louisa cleaned the area with antiseptic. He was so kind, so caring, she thought. He had so much to give. And it was time she stopped keeping him at arm's length.

When Rob and his mother left, Louisa put her hand on Dominic's arm. 'Can I have a quick word?'

He looked slightly wary. 'Sure.'

'Last night…I was a bit hasty.' She took a deep breath. 'I still don't think Ty would cope too well with a wedding, but I asked Mum and Dad if they'd have him for the day. So, if the offer's still open—yes, please, I'd love to go to the wedding with you.'

Dominic sucked in a breath. 'As my friend, or as my colleague?'

'Not as your colleague,' she said. 'Or as your "good friend".' If he was going to introduce her to his family, then they'd do it properly. 'I was thinking as your girlfriend.' She wrinkled her nose. 'Well, I'm probably a bit too old to be called a girlfriend. Partner, then.'

In response, he wrapped his arms round her and kissed her soundly.

Obviously she looked shocked, because he laughed. 'Hey. You're standing under some mistletoe.'

'No, I'm not. We don't do anything more than tinsel and cards in the admin areas and a tree in Reception, and you know it.'

'Imaginary mistletoe, then. And I should warn you that there's a lot of it about at this time of year. I might have to kiss you in all sorts of places.' His eyes glittered. 'Thank you. I know it was a big ask.'

'When is it, so I can let Mum and Dad know?'

'The Saturday after next.'

'What?' She stared at him in surprise. 'Dominic, haven't you left it a bit late? I mean, what about table plans and everything?'

'That won't be a problem. Two minutes on a computer, that's all.' He paused. 'Um, and it's not a day thing. It's a weekend.'

'A whole weekend?' She knew she was sounding like a parrot, but Dominic had left her too stunned to do anything else but repeat what he said. How could a man who was so organised at work be so hopelessly disorganised about his brother's wedding?

'Dinner with my family on Friday night,' Dominic explained, 'then the wedding itself on Saturday. And we'll stay over on Saturday night.'

'In a hotel near your family?'

'No. We'll stay at the castle.'

'Castle?'

'Amberhurst.'

She smiled. 'What a lovely setting. I didn't realise they held wedding receptions there or that you could book a room to stay there.'

'You can't.'

She frowned. 'I'm not with you. You just said your brother's getting married there.'

'It's a family tradition to marry at the church in the castle grounds and, with Oliver being the eldest son...' He shrugged. 'I guess it's the obvious place.'

She suddenly realised. 'You mean your family *owns* Amberhurst Castle?'

'Yes.'

She sat down, shaking her head in disbelief. 'Dominic, we went there for the jousting, and you never said a word.'

'I was going to tell you when we were there. I

was going to introduce you and Tyler to Oliver and my parents—but then Ty came off the pony and there just wasn't time.'

She blew out a breath. 'Dominic, what else aren't you telling me?'

'Nothing. It's not a big deal.'

'Isn't it? I feel a bit out of my depth,' she said. 'Your parents own a castle. So that means this is going to be a society wedding—and, well, you've met my family. We're not posh.'

He looked surprised. 'Your parents are lovely. And it's not about being posh or any society stuff. It's just a quiet family wedding, at my family's home. And I can assure you, you'll fit right in. Just as I do with your family.'

He scooped her up, sat down on her chair, and settled her on his lap. 'The reason I didn't ask you about the wedding earlier was because Ty was still recovering and I didn't want to put any pressure on you, in case he wasn't well enough to come. I didn't want you to feel obliged to go to the wedding because you'd accepted the invitation and then end up spending the whole time worrying yourself sick about him. And you can change your mind about him joining us at any time—even on the morning of the wedding itself. It won't be a problem for anyone.'

He really wanted her there. He wanted to introduce her to his family. As his partner. And he'd included Ty.

'Come with me,' he said softly. 'I really want you there with me.'

'OK. But I need to know the dress code,' she warned. 'And what colour the bridesmaids are wearing, so I don't clash.'

'I'll text Oliver and find out,' he said. He rested his forehead against her shoulder. 'I'm sorry I didn't tell you before. I'm not very good at timing.'

'You're telling me,' she said drily, stroking the hair back from his forehead. 'And you'd better let me go before someone walks in and catches us in a clinch. We're meant to be concentrating on our patients, Dr Hurst, not snuggling up together at my desk.'

He stole a kiss, then let her wriggle off her lap. 'I think I need you to keep me on the straight and narrow.'

'What about the wedding list?'

'I've already ordered their present. But if you

offer to wrap it for me,' he said with a smile, 'I'll be your slave. I'm hopeless at wrapping.'

'I can't imagine you being hopeless at anything,' she said drily.

And now she had to find an outfit suitable for a society wedding, and she'd have to go shopping on Saturday—the first Saturday in December, when the shops would be crowded with people brandishing Christmas lists. One of her least favourite chores. Especially as it meant that she'd miss out on spending precious weekend time with Ty.

But her mother came to the rescue. 'We'll have a look online—then I'll go into town tomorrow armed with your shortlist. You're the same size as me, so I can try them on, and I'll bring you the ones I think will suit you best and take the others back the next day.'

'You're wonderful. And I owe you a spa day,' Louisa said.

Gillian laughed. 'I'll hold you to that.'

But what her mother came up with the following day was nothing like the dresses Louisa had chosen with her on the internet. Gillian had picked a violet-coloured dress with a sweetheart neckline and strappy top, with an organza skirt that fell softly from the empire waistline almost to her ankles. There was a lilac pashmina to go with it, and an organza and feather fascinator in a perfect matching colour, and the prettiest underwear Louisa had ever seen—as well as a pair of black strappy shoes that she didn't think she'd be able to walk in, let alone dance in.

Oh, help. She hadn't even thought about dancing.

'Mum, this looks a bit...'

'I don't care. Try it on,' Gillian said firmly.

The dress fitted perfectly. The shoes were far more comfortable than they looked. And Louisa stared at herself in the mirror, surprised.

'You look gorgeous,' Gillian said. 'Wear your hair up, with a couple of strands down and curled to soften it.' She produced a box from her handbag. 'And wear Granny's pearls. They'll set this off beautifully.'

'Mum—thank you so much. You're wonderful.' Louisa hugged her. 'And I meant it about that spa day.'

'I'll look forward to that, darling.' Gillian hugged her back. 'So does this mean that we can stop pretending that you and Dominic are just good friends now?'

'We *are* good friends.'

'You're a bit more than that, love,' Gillian said.

Louisa blinked. 'How did you know?'

'Apart from the fact that mothers have a sixth sense about these things,' Gillian said drily, 'it's obvious in the way you look at each other.' She paused. 'He's a much, much better man than Jack ever was. He's reliable, he's kind and he adores Ty. I think you're good together. So does your father. And it's about time you had a bit of happiness.'

Tear pricked her eyes. 'Oh, Mum.'

'Don't,' Gillian warned, 'or I'll start crying, too, and then Ty will want to know what's wrong. Come on. Let's go and ask the boys what they think of your glad rags.' She tucked her arm into Louisa's. 'I'm so proud of you, the woman you've become. And I think Dominic's the right one. He's good enough for my girl.'

CHAPTER TEN

ON THE Friday evening of the following week, Dominic drove Louisa to Amberhurst for the pre-wedding dinner. He stopped in front of the gates, got out of the car and tapped a code into a discreet panel by the wall. The gates swung open silently and then closed again behind them as he drove through; the castle loomed in front of them.

When he eventually parked the car in front of the castle, Louisa felt as if her stomach was tied in knots. Now she had an idea how Dominic must have felt about meeting her parents. Would she measure up?

'They'll love you,' Dominic said.

She blinked. 'Did I just say that out loud?'

'Uh-huh.' He kissed her swiftly. 'Give it five minutes, and I promise you'll feel at home. My family's very normal. Well. Normal*ish*,' he amended. 'I suppose they're a bit eccentric.'

But he loved them. She could see that in

his expression. So she was prepared to love them, too.

He insisted on carrying her case as well as his own. He set them down briefly while he tapped in a code into the panel by the front door, then opened the door and toted them inside. Immediately there was a huge amount of barking and four assorted dogs burst into the hallway.

'It's OK, they won't hurt you. They're more likely to lick you to death.' He stooped down and allowed them to leap about over him, and she followed his lead.

'Oh, you horrible lot! Benjy, Cody, Buster and Fudge, *heel*.' An older woman—Louisa recognised her from the photographs in Dominic's flat as his mother—came into the hallway. She was beautifully dressed and perfectly coiffured; Louisa felt a teensy bit daunted. But she had the same smile as Dominic, and her eyes were warm as she assessed the younger woman. She kissed Dominic. 'Hello, darling.'

He kissed her back. 'Hello, Ma.'

'You're just in time.' She smiled at Louisa. 'And you must be Louisa.'

'Hello.' Louisa smiled awkwardly. 'I'm so sorry,

I'm afraid I don't know much about etiquette. Do I call you Lady Hurst? And, um, do I curtsey?'

'You call me Milly, and forget all the other nonsense.' Dominic's mother enveloped her in a hug. 'Welcome to Amberhurst, Louisa. And I'm sorry about this lot giving you such a noisy welcome.'

'It's OK. I like dogs.'

'Even Great Danes?' Milly asked, looking surprised. 'Fudge, *sit*,' she said in exasperation to the Great Dane, who'd sneaked forward and was busy sniffing Louisa's knees.

Louisa laughed and fondled the dog's ears. 'My son's desperate for a wolfhound. I've explained that we can't have a dog where we live now, but maybe one day we can have a dog. Something spaniel-sized, maybe.' She knew that Tyler would adore these four, from the little Jack Russell right up to the huge Great Dane.

'I'm sorry that Tyler wasn't able to come to the wedding,' Milly said. 'I was looking forward to meeting him. Dominic explained why and I completely understand. I remember when Andy was little; if there were too many people around it made him uncomfortable, so he'd go and sit with the dogs or the horses—and his parents used to have to go and search for him, worried sick that he'd wandered near the pond or something.' She shivered. 'Perish the thought. But maybe when it's a little quieter around here he might like to come and visit and play with the dogs.'

'Thank you. That's very kind of you.'

'Everyone's in the drawing room. Dinner's almost ready. Dominic, do you want to take the luggage upstairs? Louisa, I'm just going to give these monsters their dinner in the boot room to shut them up, but do come and have a glass of champagne.' Milly raised an eyebrow. 'Or do you need the bathroom first?'

'No, I'm fine, thank you.' Louisa couldn't help feeling a little shy, but Dominic had already started upstairs with the cases.

Awkwardly, she handed Milly the posh choc-olates she'd bought in her lunch hour. 'I, um, wanted to bring something to say thank you for having me to stay, but flowers didn't feel right—not the day before a wedding when there are going to be flowers everywhere.'

'That's so *sweet* of you, but you really didn't have to bring anything. I know I have you to thank for the smile being back behind Dominic's eyes, and that's the best gift any mother can ask for. Her child being happy.'

Just what her own mother had said. And how she knew she'd feel about Tyler's eventual choice of partner, when he grew up.

Milly looked away, but not before Louisa caught the sheen of tears in her eyes. She blinked them away rapidly and cleared her throat. 'And these are for me?' She peeked at the package and beamed. 'Oh, I *love* these. I know I'm going to like you, Louisa. A lot. You'll have to forgive me for being rude and not offering these to everyone else with coffee. These are going in my study.'

'Would that be in your "secret" chocolate drawer, Ma?' Dominic drawled as he caught them up.

'Which is kept locked.'

'And you think that's going to stop anyone?' He laughed. 'Oliver taught me how to pick that lock when I was nine. And Papa taught *him*.'

Milly rolled her eyes. 'You're terrible. The three of you. How I put up with you, I really do not know! Dominic, I'm going to give these monsters their dinner before they sneak into the kitchen and start trying to scrounge things from Cook.

Take Louisa through to the drawing room.' She shooed the dogs further along the corridor, and they bounced joyfully before her, while Dominic ushered Louisa to the drawing room.

Dominic caught Louisa's hand as they reached the doorway. 'OK?' he mouthed.

'Fine,' she mouthed back. She liked Dominic's mother, and she was pretty sure she'd like the rest of his family, too.

The room was full of people. She picked out Dominic's father and brother instantly: they both looked so like him, with the same dark hair and navy-blue eyes, and of course Oliver was the only one in a wheelchair.

Dominic carefully introduced her to everyone, including Oliver's fiancée, Mina, and her parents, plus several great-aunts and great-uncles. Louisa was aware that everyone was watching them as she was introduced to Oliver, wanting to see whether she'd be fazed by the fact that he was in a wheelchair, but she ignored the feeling of being watched and smiled at Dominic's brother before shaking his hand firmly.

Milly reappeared and handed her a glass of champagne before shepherding everyone into the dining room. The table was enormous, seating eighteen; and all the places were set. It looked exactly like one of the displays in the stately castles Tyler loved visiting, with furniture so highly polished that you could practically see your reflection in it, exquisite porcelain, solid silver cutlery and candelabra, and delicate hand-blown glasses in the deepest blue. There were flowers arranged in what looked to her like priceless antique vases, and the carpet was so thick that you actually sank into it. The walls were covered with paintings and the curtains were rich deep-blue damask. Everything screamed luxury and wealth.

And then she saw the photographs on the mantelpiece. In silver frames. A wedding photograph of Dominic's parents, graduation photographs of the boys, a photograph that was clearly celebrating Oliver and Mina's engagement, and one that looked like a multi-generational family photograph. But the photographs she really loved were the more candid shots of Dominic and Oliver as children, playing in the garden. In one, Dominic had a bucket on his head and a mop in his hand, clearly pretending that he was a knight.

'That's one of my favourites. Sir Hugo's first

outing, when he was five,' Milly said with a smile, seeing what had caught Louisa's eye. 'And I love the one in his flat of the two of you with Tyler and Pegasus.'

Louisa knew the photograph she meant. The very same photograph that had pride of place in Tyler's bedroom. 'My mum took that one at the jousting. I'll have a copy made for you, if you like.'

'Thank you. I'd love that. It's the happiest I've seen Dominic for more than two years.' Milly paused. 'We had hoped to meet you at the jousting. But then there was the accident. It must have been terrifying for you.'

'It was. I'm just so lucky Ty's made a complete recovery.' Then Louisa bit her lip, remembering Oliver—who'd also been involved in a riding accident and would never make a complete recovery. 'Sorry, that wasn't very tactful.'

'But it was honest. And Oliver does at least have most of his independence. It could have been an awful lot worse. At least I don't have to cope with an Oliver-shaped hole in my life. That would be a lot, lot harder.' Milly patted her arm.

Louisa discovered that she was seated at the

opposite end of the table from Dominic, next to Oliver.

'Can I help you at all?' she asked as Oliver prepared to transfer himself from his state-of-the-art lightweight wheelchair to the dining chair.

'Thanks, but I can manage.' He smiled at her, softening the slight abruptness of his tone. 'It was about time Dominic brought you to meet us. How's your little boy doing?'

'He's fine, thanks.'

'Is he back in the saddle yet?'

She took a deep breath. 'No. I'm not sure I'm ready for that.'

'Of course, it's your decision,' Oliver said. 'But he'll miss out on an awful lot.'

How could he say that, when he'd been so badly injured in a fall from a horse?

As if he could read her thoughts, he said softly, 'Once a horseman, always a horseman. I miss it.' He paused, his eyes growing serious. 'Dominic said he told you about the accident.'

'Yes.'

Oliver looked relieved. 'I'm glad he's talking about it. He refused counselling afterwards, but I think he needed it as much as I did. More than I did, probably. I used to play rugby, and I could've had a bad tackle at any time that would've left me like this. I wouldn't have held it against the person who tackled me, and I don't hold this against my brother.'

'He does enough of that for himself,' Louisa agreed.

He gave her a level look. 'Maybe you're the one who can help him learn to forgive himself. Because it wasn't his fault. It was a stupid accident, and I'm just as much to blame because I wasn't giving the joust my full concentration. I've told him that, but it didn't stop him wearing a hair shirt.' He sighed. 'I'm half-surprised he didn't decide to train as a surgeon to make up for the fact that I'm not one any more. But it'd be a waste if he did—emergency medicine suits him down to the ground.'

'He's an excellent doctor. And he said you were a brilliant surgeon.'

'I was,' Oliver said, with no hint of arrogance— just like Dominic, she thought, Oliver would make enough effort to excel at anything he did. 'But now I intend to be a brilliant GP. I'm retraining. So I'll still get to make patients better—but

I'll get to see my patients over the whole of their treatment rather than simply fixing a valve in their heart and waving them off home to recuperate and having no idea whether their lives really are better after the op. And the hours are more family-friendly, which Mina will appreciate—I can do my fair share of changing nappies.' He shrugged. 'If life gives you lemons, you'd better learn to make lemonade—or you're going to wallow in misery, and I can tell you from experience that that's a complete waste of time.'

Milly made everyone change places between courses, so over the next course Louisa ended up sitting next to Roderick, Dominic and Oliver's father, who was incredibly sweet; and over pudding she was charmed by their great-uncles, Rupert and Ashton. After dinner, the women all withdrew to the drawing room again, leaving the men to their port; Louisa finally got to chat to Mina, Oliver's fiancée, who turned out to be incredibly sweet-natured. She and Oliver would definitely be happy together, Louisa thought.

When the men joined them again, Dominic sat on the arm of Louisa's chair, resting his hand on the nape of her neck. Although she knew this was all for show and didn't actually mean anything, she still couldn't help the little thrill running through her at his touch.

Finally people started drifting off to bed.

'Can I help you clear up?' Louisa asked Milly.

'It's all taken care of,' Milly said with a smile.

Of course. To run a house this size, they'd need staff. And Milly had mentioned a cook, earlier.

'But bless you for offering.' Milly gave her a hug. 'We've got a busy day tomorrow. I think we all need to try and get some sleep.'

'Yes. Goodnight,' Louisa said politely.

'I'll see you up,' Dominic said.

'I had a lovely evening,' she said as they walked up the sweeping central staircase. 'I like your family.'

'Good. They liked you, too.' He paused outside a door that she assumed led to her room. 'Um, there's something I need to talk to you about. Can we go inside?'

'Sure.'

He opened the door and flicked on the light.

What she saw was a very masculine room—and her case was standing right next to Dominic's.

He looked awkward. 'I thought you were going to be in the room next door to mine, but we have the great-aunts staying and there was a burst pipe yesterday that's made two of the bedrooms un-inhabitable, which means we're shorter on space than usual. I'm afraid my mother made a bit of an assumption. She's put us both in my room.'

Meaning that his mother thought they were already sleeping together. Louisa felt the colour shoot into her face. 'Oh.'

'Look, I've got a blanket in the back of the car—I'll go and fetch it. I can sleep on the floor.'

'Dominic.' She placed her hand on his arm before he could open the bedroom door again. 'I'm not going to make you sleep on the floor. We can share a room.'

Colour rose in his face. 'This wasn't some deep, dark plot, you know. I wasn't intending to share a bed with you this weekend. Actually, I'd been planning to take you to Venice in April. The most romantic city in the world, in springtime. And *then* I was going to seduce you.'

'April. That's quite a long time to wait.'

He shrugged. 'You're worth waiting for.'

She could see in his eyes that he meant it. And it melted her. 'Maybe it's time we stopped waiting.'

He sucked in a breath. 'Are you sure about that?'

'Very sure,' she said softly. She tipped her head back so that she could look at him. Lord, he was gorgeous. His pupils were so huge that his eyes looked black, there was the faintest shadow of stubble on his face, and that beautiful mouth… How could she resist?

'You're beautiful. Adorable,' he said softly, and bent his head. He brushed his mouth against hers, and when she leaned into him he caught her lower lip between his, teasing it and cajoling her into letting him deepen the kiss.

Desire spun through her; Dominic was irresistible. And, best of all, he was all hers.

He stroked his fingers under along the bare skin of her back, above the top of her dress. 'Your skin's so soft,' he said, his voice full of wonder. 'Louisa, I really need to touch you.'

She needed him to touch her, too; she could feel her nipples hardening and her breasts were aching. 'Then touch me,' she whispered. 'Please.' Just so he knew this was completely mutual and he wasn't pushing her into anything she didn't already want.

His hands were shaking as he lowered the zip and slid the straps from her shoulders. He dipped his head to nuzzle the skin of her shoulders, making her shiver in delight. She arched against him and his mouth traced a path of kisses along the column of her throat, then slowly along her jaw and up to her mouth, He kissed her again, his mouth sweet and sensual and offering more and more pleasure. She slid her hands into his hair and kissed him back.

He eased the bodice of her dress down towards her waist and his hand skimmed her midriff. She closed her eyes as his hand slip up further underneath and at last he cupped her breast, teasing the hard peak of her nipple between his forefinger and thumb and rubbing it against the lace of her bra.

He broke the kiss, his breathing uneven. 'Louisa, I want to see you.'

She knew what he was asking, and nodded. He slowly eased her dress over her hips, and she shimmied until the material hit the floor. There was a deep, intense look in his eyes as he un-hooked her bra and let the lacy garment fall.

And then he looked.

He sucked in a breath. 'You're gorgeous.'

Desire kicked sharply through her. 'I need to see you, too.'

'I'm in your hands.'

Slowly, she removed his tie. Opened the buttons of his shirt, very, very slowly. Pushed the soft cotton off his shoulders. And stared.

It was the first time she'd ever seen him stripped to the waist; there was light sprinkling of hair over his chest, and he had perfect six-pack abs, which she knew came from riding and working in the stables rather than from pumping iron in a gym.

Feeling brave enough to touch him back, now, she stroked his pectoral muscles. 'You look like a Greek god.'

He laughed. 'Hardly. I'm just a man.'

Just? she thought. No, Dominic wasn't 'just' anything. He was special. And she loved him. Really, really loved him.

Not that she could scare him by telling him that.

Not now, when they were going to make love for the first time. Better to concentrate on a different truth: the fact that she really, really wanted him. Physically, he blew her mind.

She reached up and pressed a kiss against his chest, and he gave a sharp intake of breath. 'Do you have any idea how much I want you?'

'About as much as I want you, hopefully.'

His eyes widened. 'Oh, yes. I want you *now*,' he said hoarsely.

Common sense was forgotten; all she knew was that she needed this man to touch her and make her see stars. 'Yes.'

He dipped his head and kissed her throat in a way that made her arch back against him. He drew a line of kisses along her collar-bone, teasing the pulse-point and making her wriggle, and then slowly, slowly moved downwards. His mouth was warm and sweet against her skin, making her want more. Then, at long last, he closed his mouth over her nipple, sucking hard. She gasped his name in pleasure and slid her fingers into his hair, urging him on.

After that, things went blank for a while. She had no idea which of them moved first, which of them finished undressing the other, but then they were skin to skin, and it felt so good.

'If you want me to stop,' he said huskily, 'say it now and I'll go and have a cold shower.'

'If you stop now,' she said, 'I think I'll go insane.'

He smiled. 'You and me both, honey.' He stroked her thighs apart, and sucked in a breath. 'Your skin's so soft.' He cupped her sex, and she pushed against him.

'Don't tease.'

He pushed a finger into her, circling her clitoris with his thumb.

She closed her eyes and a breath shuddered from her. 'Oh, that's good. Oh, Dominic. *Yes.*'

'Mmm. You're so responsive.' He stole a kiss, then kissed a path down her body. Her hands fisted in his hair as she felt his mouth on her, just where she needed it most.

Her orgasm surprised her, unexpectedly fast and fierce, and she gasped.

'OK?' he asked, looking concerned.

'Yes, I… It's been a while,' she admitted. 'I'm a bit out of practice.'

'You're delightful,' he told her. 'Sexy as hell. And I really, really want to make love with you.'

'Yes,' she breathed. 'Yes, please.'

He took his wallet from the table next to the bed and removed a condom; he ripped open the foil packet and rolled the condom onto his penis, then kissed her again, his kiss sweet and yearning. At last, he fitted the tip of his penis against her and slowly eased into her.

'Dominic.' She stroked his face. She knew he was holding back, being gentle with her—but gentle wasn't enough right now. 'I want all of you.' She shifted so she could wrap her legs round his waist.

Dominic could hardly believe that this warm, generous woman wanted him as badly as he wanted her. He felt as if he was losing himself in Louisa. Her warm sweet depths were wrapped round him, her eyes were all dark with desire, and he couldn't resist dipping his head to steal a kiss. She slid her hands into his hair, drawing him closer, and kissed him back.

It was as if stars were exploding inside his head

as he felt her body ripple round his, urging him on towards his own climax. He'd never felt anything quite like this before, such a pure and deep connection. All he could do was hold on.

But when his pulse had finally slowed to normal, guilt kicked in.

'I'm sorry. I shouldn't have taken advantage of you.'

Her legs were still wrapped round his waist, and she refused to let him go. 'You didn't take advantage of me. I was there with you, all the way.'

'This was supposed to be Venice in April. A four-poster bed, candlelight and Bellinis. I wanted to make it really romantic.'

'Some people,' she said softly, 'would think that an ancient castle is just as romantic. Including me.' She stroked his face. 'I wanted this as much as you did. And I've already made you wait for long enough.'

'You're incredible. You make me feel as if I can conquer the world.'

'You can.' She stole a kiss. 'And you don't feel quite so tense now. Are you still worried about tomorrow?'

'Being Oliver's best man? Yes and no.' He sighed. 'I mean, Mina loves him to bits. She's stood by him, even when he went through the ragingly angry stage and tried to push her away. Getting married is absolutely the right thing for them to do. But he's not going to be able to walk down the aisle with her. He's not going to be able to carry her over the threshold. It's things like that I feel I've stolen from his future.'

'He doesn't blame you. He told me last night, apart from the fact he thinks he contributed to it himself, it could've happened in a rugby match. And he really doesn't hold it against you. You're the only one doing that.' She paused. 'And you've given him something else. Did you know he's retraining?'

'No.' Oliver hadn't breathed a word to him. Given the state of his back, it had to be a desk job. 'What's he doing, taking over the estate management from Papa or something?'

'He's going to be a GP. So he gets to care for his patients all the way through. And, as he put it, it's family-friendly hours.'

'He's planning to have a family?' Dominic really hadn't expected that.

'Put it this way, he was talking about changing nappies. And whether they're able to have children of their own, or they need IVF or they decide to adopt, I think Oliver's going to be a very hands-on dad.' She stroked his hair away from his forehead. 'He reminds me a lot of you. He's got that same energy.'

'Yes.' And he wanted to be a hands-on dad, too. With a ready-made family—and maybe a little brother or sister for Tyler. And a puppy. A house, a garden, a family: Tyler's dream definitely matched his, and he hoped that it matched Louisa's, too.

Not that he intended to propose to her in bed. Or right now. He hadn't even told her he loved her—though he had a feeling that she might already have guessed that.

He kissed the tip of her nose. 'Though there's something I should tell you, Nurse Practitioner Austin. I'm really looking forward to falling asleep with you in my arms. And waking up with you.'

'Guess what?' Her face was all soft and sweet. 'I'm looking forward to that, too.'

And suddenly his plans for Venice didn't matter any more. Because this was just perfect. Everything he wanted.

CHAPTER ELEVEN

THE next morning, Louisa woke, feeling all warm and cosy, to find herself sprawled all over Dominic. Her head was on his shoulder, her arm was round his waist and her fingers were curving down over his hipbone. Her legs were tangled with his; and his arms were wrapped tightly round her.

'Good morning,' he said softly.

She felt herself flush. 'Have you been awake for long?'

'Long enough to enjoy you sleeping. You're delectable. And I love the way your skin feels against mine.' He shifted so he could kiss her. 'All's very right with my world this morning.'

So he'd stopped panicking about being Oliver's best man? Good. Hopefully he was finally starting to forgive himself.

'Does your hair take hideously long to dry?' he asked.

'Not if you have a hairdryer I can borrow.'

'Good.' He kissed her again. 'Because I really need to introduce you to my shower.' Three seconds later, he scooped her out of bed and carried her into the shower, laughing.

This was something she would never have done with Jack. And yet, with Dominic, it felt right. The intensity in his eyes when he looked at her, the sheer desire on his face: they sent a thrill through her. And was she deluding herself, or was it more than just desire? Could Dominic feel the same way about her that she felt about him? Did he love her back? The possibility shimmered in the air.

They spent longer in the shower than Dominic had planned and it was a rush to get her hair dried, but finally they made it downstairs. Louisa was glad to help out with all the last-minute tasks and checking to make sure that all the arrangements for the wedding were going smoothly. The flowers were breathtaking—the bold, clean lines of the calla lilies softened by the pretty star-shaped flowers of the tuberoses—and the marquee was filled with staff, setting the tables and checking the table plans and putting the place-holders in the right places.

Milly sent Dominic off with the dogs, saying that he needed to burn off some of his energy before he drove her insane with all that pacing around; and Louisa was drafted in to help amuse the five-year-old flower girl and three-year-old pageboy, telling them stories and teaching them new songs.

And then finally it was time to get ready for the ceremony. Dominic stared as Louisa emerged from the bathroom in her dress. 'You look fantastic,' he said.

'Don't sound so surprised,' she said drily.

'Sorry, I didn't mean to insult you. What I meant was, apart from last night, I've only ever seen you either in uniform at work or wearing jeans. You look lovely.'

'Thank you. You look pretty amazing yourself,' she said. Formal dress suited him; and when he gave her a shy smile her heart skipped a beat.

'Do you have a wrap or something?' he asked. 'The church can get pretty chilly.'

She nodded, and fished out the lilac pashmina. He draped it round her shoulders. 'I really like your hair like that, too.' He dipped his head and kissed the back of her neck; the touch of his lips against her skin made a shiver of desire ripple all the way down her spine. 'Sorry,' he said. 'There's just something about you that I can't resist.'

The compliment made her glow, and she tucked her hand into the crook of his arm as they left the room and headed downstairs.

'You look fabulous, Louisa,' Milly said. 'That colour really suits you.'

'Thank you. You look lovely, too,' Louisa said, meaning it.

Milly was wearing a suit in sky-blue silk, with a matching hat and a corsage of tuberoses. She took another corsage from the box resting on one of the little tables in the hallway and pinned it to Louisa's dress.

'Thank you. They smell gorgeous,' Louisa said, breathing in the heady, exotic scent.

'Don't they just?' Milly smiled. 'So clever of Mina to choose them.'

Milly handed her a buttonhole for Dominic, a single calla lily, and Louisa carefully pinned it onto his lapel.

Roderick emerged from the kitchen. Milly

cuffed his arm and wiped the tell-tale crumbs from the corner of his mouth. 'Honestly, *men*! Do they never stop eating?' she asked, rolling her eyes.

'I was hungry,' Roderick protested, 'and you know what it's like at weddings. It takes ages before anybody gets fed, what with the photographs and the receiving lines and all that hanging around.'

'Just *behave*,' Milly said—and Louisa could see exactly where Dominic had got his irresistible little-boy grin.

Oliver was the last to arrive in the hallway, wheeling himself down the corridor.

Louisa saw the stricken look in Dominic's eyes, and slipped her fingers through his, squeezing his hand gently. 'Smile,' she said softly. 'Everything's just fine.'

He gave her a grateful glance and did so.

'So are we all ready now?' Milly asked, deftly pinning on Oliver's buttonhole.

'I'm nervous,' Oliver admitted, 'but I'm ready. Because Mina's about to make me the happiest man in the world when she walks down the aisle to me.'

Everyone else was looking at Oliver, but Louisa was looking at Dominic—and she saw him flinch. And, as they walked to the church, she noticed his steps starting to drag as they drew nearer.

'I think I need a breath of fresh air,' she said as they reached the beautiful old building. 'Dominic, would you mind...?'

'Of course,' he said, and stepped to the side with her. 'Are you all right?' he asked quietly.

She waited until his parents and Oliver had gone inside. 'I'm fine, but you're not. Talk to me.'

He rested his head against the cold stone of the porch. 'This is all so *wrong*. Oliver should be walking down that aisle, not wheeling himself down it. How can I possibly be his best man when I did that to him?'

'We talked about this last night. It was an *accident*. Oliver's come to terms with the situation,' Louisa said softly. 'Now you need to do the same. There's nothing you can do to change it, so just try to make the best of it. Do you know what he said to me last night? If life gives you lemons, you have to make lemonade. And he's right. Look at the good bits. Your family's lovely. They adore you—including Oliver—and that's why he asked you to be his best man. Nobody else will do. And today's a really, really special day.'

'You're right,' he said, taking a deep breath. 'It's Oliver's day, and I need to put the past and the might-have-beens out of my head. And thank you for stopping me acting like a selfish jerk.'

'You're welcome,' she said.

He was still holding her hand when they walked into the church. It was full of white flowers, and the sun shone through the stained-glass windows, dappling the flowers with rich jewelled tones. The perfect winter wedding: all they needed was a tiny sprinkle of snow after the service, to act as confetti, she thought with a smile.

The tiny church soon filled up, and then the organist started to play the Trumpet Voluntary. All chatter ceased and everyone stood up, turning round to look at Mina. She looked amazing, walk-ing down the red carpet in the aisle on her father's arm, the bridesmaids and flower girl and pageboy behind her. She joined Oliver at the top of the aisle; the vicar made the introductory speech, and when it came to the vows Oliver hauled himself out of his wheelchair. Clearly it was a struggle for him—Louisa could see the flash of pain across his face—but he was obviously determined to say his wedding vows to his bride while standing on his own two feet.

Louisa held Dominic's hand really tightly, and there wasn't a dry eye in the congregation as Mina and Oliver made their vows and he kissed her before lowering himself back into his wheelchair. She could see Dominic blinking back tears when he returned to the pew after handing the rings over, and the lump in her throat grew even bigger when a woman started playing a violin solo and then a man with a gorgeous tenor voice started singing Louis Armstrong's 'Wonderful World' while Mina and Oliver signed the register.

The next few hours passed in a blur. Photographs, the champagne reception, a gorgeous meal and then the speeches. Dominic gave a very funny speech that had everyone laughing. But then he grew serious.

'I've always looked up to my big brother, right from the first moment I was able to toddle along behind him. Oliver's an amazing man, full of courage and strength and kindness, and I couldn't have wished for a better role model. I'm incredibly proud of him.' Dominic's voice cracked slightly.

'And I love him very, very much. So I'd like you all to join with me in wishing him and my new sister-in-law every happiness for the future.' He raised his glass. 'The bride and groom.'

When Louisa glanced over at Roderick and Milly, she could see them both wiping away a tear as they raised their glasses. And there was a suspicious sheen in everyone else's eyes, too, as they raised their glasses and echoed Dominic's toast.

'That was a beautiful speech,' she whispered to him, 'and you've really done your family proud.'

He said nothing, but held her hand very tightly through the rest of the speeches. Particularly when Oliver looked him straight in the eye during his speech and said, 'And I'd like to thank my best man. He's given me more than he knows, over the years, and I couldn't have asked for a better brother. I've been truly blessed in my family— and I'm so glad I can share that blessing with the love of my life, too.'

It was a public declaration from both of them. But would it be enough to break through the barriers Dominic had put round his heart? Louisa wondered. He'd heard his brother's speech, but had he listened to it—really listened to it—and understood that it was time to let the past go?

His face gave nothing away; and now wasn't the time or place for her to ask.

And finally it was time for the first dance.

Louisa had half-wondered if they'd skip the dancing, but clearly Oliver had other ideas. And when Dominic ushered her away from the table, she realised that the marquee led into the ball-room, where a band was set up at one corner.

They began to play the first notes of a song she recognised.

'"You Raise Me Up". What a fantastic song for a first dance,' she said. 'The lyrics give me goose bumps every time.'

It was a very, very, very slow dance, but Oliver and Mina managed it. And at the end of the dance, everyone cheered the bride and groom. Dominic had his arms wrapped round Louisa and was holding her really close; she could feel the tension running through him.

'You're supposed to dance with the chief brides-maid now,' Louisa reminded him gently, 'while your mum dances with Mina's dad and her mum dances with your dad.'

'Yes, of course.' He shook himself.

'Go and be the gorgeous, charming man you are. For Oliver and Mina,' she said softly.

'As long as you promise to dance with me for the rest of the evening.'

She brushed a kiss against his lips and smiled at him. 'Absolutely.'

Dominic did exactly as Louisa had suggested. He danced with Mina's sister, chatted normally to her—and he was able to be charming, and all because he knew Louisa was waiting for him. With her, he felt different. He felt like a better person, not just the man who'd changed his brother and his family's life for ever. When he'd listened to the words of the song Oliver and Mina had chosen for the first dance, he'd realised that they fitted the way he felt about Louisa, too. She made him more than he thought he could be.

When the song ended, he noticed that his brother was sitting down; not so unusual, but there was a tightening round his eyes that made Dominic suspect Oliver was in an awful lot of pain. Quietly, he went over to him. 'Are you all right?' he asked, concerned.

'I just got married. I'm more than OK. And I had the first dance with my beautiful bride. That was the one that mattered.' Oliver smiled at him. 'I know what you're worrying about. Don't. All that physio and work in the swimming pool paid off. I'm not going to be stuck in bed for a week, recovering.'

'You're in pain right now.'

Oliver shrugged. 'It's worth it.'

Dominic took his hand. 'Oliver, I'm so—'

'Shh,' Oliver said. 'I know. And I'm fine—really, Dominic, I'm fine. I've been training with my physio for that dance for months, so I haven't knocked myself up. And I'm still going to carry my bride over the threshold tonight, except she's going to be sitting on my lap as I carry her.'

Guilt squeezed Dominic's heart.

'Dominic, listen to me. I'm not sitting here thinking about what I don't have—I'm sitting here, truly thankful for what I do have. This is my perfect day. I've just got married to the woman I love most in the world, in the place I love most in the world, with all the people I love around me.

And I'm about to start a new career as a GP. I've got so much ahead of me, so much good stuff to come.' He paused. 'The past is the past. It's time you let it go, little brother.'

'How can I?' Dominic asked.

'Listen to your girl. She talks a lot of sense.'

'She talks a lot, full stop,' Dominic said wryly.

Oliver laughed. 'Then, between the pair of you, I bet it's hard to get a word in edgeways.'

'She lets me be silent, too,' Dominic mused. And it was true. With Louisa, he'd discovered that he could be himself. She knew the worst of him, and yet she hadn't pushed him away. If anything, she'd drawn him closer.

'She's lovely. And I'm glad you've found some-one, Dominic. I've hated seeing you slowly shut-ting yourself off from people these past two years.'

'She's special,' Dominic said softly. 'Really special.'

'Be happy. That's all I want for you,' Oliver said, 'to be as happy as I am. Now go and dance with your girl before we both get maudlin.' Oliver smiled at him. 'And, just for the record,

I meant everything I said in my speech. I'm proud of you.'

'I love you, Oliver,' Dominic said.

'I know. And I love you, too.' Oliver returned his hug, then patted his back. 'Go and dance with lovely Louisa. And stop worrying about me. *Really.*'

The band was playing 'The Way You Look Tonight'. Another song with more than appropriate words. There really was nobody like Louisa in the room. And the way she looked tonight... that'd stay with him for a long, long time.

Dominic went to claim his dance with her, and found himself singing along with the song.

'Why, Dr Hurst, I didn't know you had such a nice singing voice. Or that a die-hard rock fan like you would know the words to a Sinatra song.' Her eyes were sparkling.

'I grew up with this stuff.'

'My parents are more into the Beatles,' she said, 'though Mum once admitted that she had a crush on Andy Williams.'

'"Can't Take My Eyes Off You". That's one of Ma's favourites, too, though I prefer the Muse version,' he said reflectively. 'It has better guitars.'

She laughed. 'You *would* say that.'

Then the band switched to another slow number, Dominic drew Louisa close, swaying with her to the rhythm of the song. She wasn't wearing her wrap, so her shoulders were bare except for the two tiny straps. Unable to resist, he dipped his head and kissed her shoulder. Her skin was so soft and she smelled so sweet.

She gave a breathy little sigh and moved closer; and he felt his control fraying past the point of no return. He needed her, and he couldn't help himself; he traced a path of kisses up the sensitive cord at the side of her neck, drawing her closer still, and then finally his mouth was right where he wanted it to be, jammed over hers. Her arms were round his neck and she was kissing him back, her mouth warm and sweet and promising.

Heaven.

It took him a while to realise that the band were playing a more up-tempo number. He had no idea how long he'd been kissing Louisa on the dance floor; the only thing he knew was that he didn't want to stop—and he didn't want an audience.

'Louisa,' he whispered as he broke the kiss.

She looked dazed. 'Hmm?'

'There's something I need to tell you.' And he knew where, too. 'Let's go,' he said. 'Somewhere a little quieter. More private.'

She gave him the most sinful smile. 'What a good idea.'

It was all he could do not to turn caveman, haul her over his shoulder and carry her upstairs to his bed. But they left the ballroom discreetly. He led her down a corridor and out through a side door into the formal garden. 'Look up,' he said.

'Wow. I don't think I've ever seen stars that bright.' She smiled. 'And a full moon, too. It's pure silver.'

And the soft light made her look incredibly beautiful. He took off his jacket and slipped it round her shoulders.

She looked concerned. 'You'll be cold, Dominic.'

'I'm with you. So I'm warm where it matters.' He took her hand and placed it over his heart. 'Right here. Feel?'

'Yes.' She smiled at him.

'I love you, Louisa,' he said softly. 'I love everything you are. And it's not just that I'm being all sentimental after seeing my big brother get married. I've known it for a while—it was just a matter of finding the right place and the right time to tell you. And that's here and now. I love you.'

'Oh, Dominic.' Her eyes glittered in the moonlight. 'I love you, too. I never expected to feel that way again, but with you it's different. You make me feel…' She shook her head. 'I can't explain it. Not properly. But everything sparkles when you're around.'

Gently, he drew her back indoors, then scooped her up and carried her up the stairs. The second he'd closed his bedroom door behind her, he let her slide down her body until her feet were back on the floor and then kissed her again, this time more passionately. And then he realised that his curtains were still open. Unwilling to relinquish her, he danced with her to the window, humming 'Can't take my eyes off you', and shut the world out.

And then he had the sheer pleasure of undressing her, very slowly. He unzipped her dress and drew a line of kisses all the way down her spine as the material parted beneath his hands, then hung her dress over the back of a chair to stop it creasing.

Louisa undressed him just as slowly, stroking the skin on his chest and his midriff as she undid his shirt, and causing his blood pressure to spike as she released the button on his trousers.

He removed the final scraps of her underwear, loving the contrast between the roughness of the lace and the softness of her skin, then scooped one arm under her knees, picking her up so he could kiss her and carry her over to his bed.

She breathed his name as he laid her against the pillows, her face filled with desire and something else he knew now he could dare to name. And he knew that he felt it, too. He could let himself love Louisa. He could be himself with her. Give her all that he wanted to be.

He paused to slide on a condom, then knelt between her thighs. 'I love you,' he said as he eased into her. 'I really, really love you.'

'And I love you. You amaze me,' she said. 'I love who you are. Your gentleness and your strength. Even your stubbornness.'

He laughed. 'I'm not the only one who's stubborn.'

'Mule. That's me,' she teased.

He kissed her. 'You're the sexiest woman I've ever met—and you turn me on in a big way, my lady.'

'"My verray, parfit, gentil knight",' she quoted. 'Do you have any idea how gorgeous you look, dressed up like a medieval prince?'

'Any time you want me dressed up in my armour, honey, just say. As long as you take it off for me again. And grant me some very special private favours.' He pushed deeper into her.

'Oh, yes.' Her expression went starry. 'And that velvet cloak. I love that cloak. I've had some seriously X-rated fantasies about you in that cloak.'

'Good. Tell me about them,' he said softly. 'Because I think I'd enjoy acting them out.'

'Kiss me,' she whispered, and he dipped his head. Her mouth was so sweet, so soft and giving. So hot. And how good she felt wrapped around him like this; the feel of her skin against his made his blood heat.

He felt her body begin to ripple round his, and he broke the kiss. 'I love you, Louisa,' he whispered.

'I love you, too.' And he could see it in her eyes,

at the exact moment that they both tumbled to a climax.

Afterwards, snuggled in bed beside her, he said, 'I don't think I've ever, ever been this happy.' He drew her close. 'I don't want tonight to end.'

'Neither do I.' She pressed a kiss into his chest. 'But I have to go home tomorrow.'

Back to real life. Yeah, he knew that.

But she'd said the words he'd needed to hear. She felt the same way as he did.

And he could risk a future with her.

CHAPTER TWELVE

THE next morning, after breakfast, Louisa was surprised when Dominic took a slightly different route from the one she'd expected.

'Aren't we going to pick Ty up?' she asked.

'Yes—but there's something I need to sort out on the way. I promise this will only take ten minutes.'

Fair enough, she thought—until she recognised the road. 'We're going to the stables?'

'Yup.'

'Dominic, you haven't ignored everything I said and arranged to meet Tyler here, have you?'

'No. This is just you and me. Ten minutes.' He parked, and took her over to the stable yard. 'Would I be right in thinking that you're just a little bit nervous of horses—and I mean in addition to the fact that you're terrified Ty's going to get hurt again?'

'Well—yes,' she admitted.

'And you've never ridden a horse?'

'Never.'

'So you don't actually know what he sees in them, do you?'

She wrapped her arms round herself. 'Why are we here?'

'Because I want to demonstrate something to you. Do you trust me?'

'Of course I do.'

'Good. Because you're going to ride my horse.'

Her mouth fell open in shock. 'But Pegasus is huge!'

'He's a gentle giant, and he's absolutely not going to hurt you. And I'm not going to let anything happen to you.'

'But I'm not dressed for horse-riding.'

'Your boots are low-heeled and you're wearing jeans and a sweater. That's fine.' He let his gaze travel all the way down from her eyes to her toes, and all the way up again. 'You look as sexy as hell, but I promise not to let myself get distracted by what I want to do to you in a quiet corner of a hayloft.'

'Dominic!' She felt the colour shoot into her face.

He grinned. 'Just giving you some ideas.' He

took her to the tack room, picked up his bridle and saddle, and took her over to Pegasus's loose box. Swiftly, he put the bridle and saddle on the horse, checked the girth, and led the horse out into the yard. 'All righty. Let me help you up. Put your left foot in the stirrup, here,' he directed. 'On the count of three, I'll help lift you up—just bring your right leg out behind you.'

The next thing she knew, she was sitting in the saddle; though she could still feel the warmth of Dominic's hands against her body, even through her clothes.

'Just relax,' he said. 'I'm leading him, so he's not going to rush off and you're not going to fall. Let yourself feel his rhythm and go along with him.'

In other words, she had to trust him.

She knew that he was a perfectionist and would never let anything go wrong. And she knew him, soul-deep. The slightly reserved and formidable doctor whose mind worked so quickly and who was so good with patients; the wild horseman with a dangerous, thrill-seeking hobby; the kind, considerate man who saw what needed fixing and just did it without a fuss; the man who treated her son as someone who was special on his own terms, not just a boy with special needs.

She loved him. Of course she trusted him.

As he slowly led her round the field, her confidence grew; and suddenly she could understand why he did this. It was a feeling like nothing else, a bond between human and horse. Shyly, she reached out to pat the horse's neck.

When they were back to their starting point, Dominic helped her down from the saddle. 'Well?'

'I get it,' she said. 'OK. You win. Ty can come back to lessons—and to the Christmas party at the stables.'

'It's not a question of winning,' Dominic said gently. 'It's about the fact that you're scared and I wanted to take the fear away. I understand why you're worried, but I wanted you to see the other side of the argument for yourself. So you could make an informed decision. The person I want to win is *you*. I don't want you all tense and worrying yourself sick every time Tyler goes on a horse—or hating yourself for being so scared about the risks that you're stopping him doing something he loves. And it occurred to me this morning that the way to beat a fear is to face it.'

'I think I'm always going to have my heart in my mouth,' she said. 'When you ride, as well as Tyler. But I understand where you're coming from now. And I'll do my best to fight the fear. To trust you'll both be safe.'

He stole a kiss. 'Good.' He made a fuss of his horse, then removed his tack and put him back in the loosebox before scooping up the saddle again. 'I'll put this back in the tack room for now. And I'll be back later to give you a proper workout,' he told Pegasus.

The horse whickered, then nosed Louisa.

Gently, she stroked his nose. 'Oh! He feels like velvet.' Entranced, she stroked him again, and the horse gave a small whicker of pleasure.

'He's an old softie.' Dominic stole a kiss. 'Come on. We need to get you back to Ty.'

On the day of the Christmas party, Dominic took Tyler and Louisa over to the stables. The yard looked amazingly festive, with a beautiful Christmas tree in the corner covered with lights.

'No tinsel, mind. It's too tempting for the ponies,' Bea said, 'and I'm not risking any holly leaves getting between a saddle and pony's back, so the tree's the only thing we do here.'

'It looks lovely, though.' Louisa produced a box. 'Sausage rolls and brownies, as promised by Dominic.'

'I helped make them,' Tyler added. 'No nuts and lots of chocolate. In the brownies, that is. The sausage rolls just have sausage in them.'

'Excellent,' Bea said, smiling. 'Thank you very much.' She led them over to the table and added the food to the already mountainous spread.

'Wow. Nobody's going to want to eat for a week afterwards,' Louisa said.

'Don't you believe it,' Bea told her, laughing. 'We always use disposable plates and cups. I know it's not as eco-friendly as washing things up, but if someone drops something it's not a problem and we don't have to worry that we've missed a bit of glass or china that'll go straight through a dog's paw or a horse's foot.'

'Very sensible.'

Bea hugged Tyler. 'Great to see you back. Polo missed you—and so did we. Your mum tells me you're starting again just after Christmas. Cool.'

'I can't wait,' Tyler said. 'And Mum says I'm allowed to do what everyone else does today.'

'Glad to hear it.'

When the party started, Louisa was absolutely charmed. Just as Dominic had described, all the children were wearing foam antlers on top of their hard hats, and they all had a turn riding the ponies round the paddock, their little antlers nodding as they rode. And Tyler's smile was the brightest of all. She was glad she'd come; she wouldn't have missed this for the world.

'This is the best Christmas party I've ever been to,' Tyler confided when everyone was happily munching mince pies. He hugged her. 'I love you, Mum.'

She felt the tears well up. Tyler didn't often make emotional statements, but when he did they always went straight to her heart. 'I love you, too,' she said, hugging him back equally hard.

'And I love Dominic.'

She went very still.

'He loves me, too. He told me when I was

ill after the accident,' Tyler said. 'Where's he gone?'

'I don't know. Probably to see Pegasus.'

But then she heard the sound of sleigh bells and she realised exactly where Dominic was. Something else he'd forgotten to mention, but something that was utterly perfect: his own role in the Christmas party.

'Father Christmas, I presume?' she asked Bea.

'Absolutely,' Bea said with a smile. 'And you wait to see what he comes in on.'

Louisa was expecting a sleigh, and maybe Bea and Ric knew someone who could bring reindeer for the children to ooh and aah over—but what she saw at the far end of the paddock was Father Christmas riding on…

'A unicorn?' she asked in disbelief. It was a pure white horse with a rippling mane and tail that looked as if it was bathed in moonlight, shimmering, and an iridescent horn coming out of his head.

Of course it wasn't a unicorn—she knew unicorns didn't exist.

But this one looked so real.

'How?' she asked in wonder.

'State secret,' Bea said with a grin. 'It's more than my life's worth to say.'

As Father Christmas rode nearer, Louisa recognised the horse as Pegasus. And when Father Christmas asked for a helper, she stepped forward. 'Will I do?'

'Perfectly,' Dominic said, handing her the first present from his sack.

There was a present for every child from the horse they rode; and Louisa loved the gift tags, which were pictures of the horses wearing Santa hats, obviously done with the help of a computer programme. The children were delighted with their gifts—all horse related—and Tyler was thrilled to bits to be given his own grooming mitt. 'This is the best Christmas ever,' he said, beaming.

Much later that evening, when Tyler was in bed, Dominic sat on the sofa with Louisa on his lap, their arms wrapped round each other.

'He's right, you know—this is going to be the best Christmas ever. Because you're in my life. You fit every bit of me: work, the stables, home. All of it.' He paused. 'What I said, the night of the wedding: I meant it. You're amazing. And I love you. And I want to be a family with you— you *and* Tyler.'

'That's what I want, too,' she said.

'But it's only going to work,' he said, 'if Tyler's happy about it.'

'He told me today that he loved you. And that you'd told him you loved him, when he was ill.' She stroked his face. 'I had no idea. Why didn't you say?'

'Because I didn't want to pressure you,' Dominic said simply. 'And, I know it's selfish, but I needed to know that you loved me for *me*, not because of the bond between me and your son.'

'I love you for both reasons. But primarily for you,' she confirmed, kissing him. 'In fact…let me show you.'

They ended up falling off the sofa, their clothing in utter disarray, but both of them were laughing.

'I feel like a teenager,' Dominic said. 'Even though I'm half a lifetime away from that.'

'Half your life ago, you were in your mid-teens,' she pointed out. 'As was I. We're both older and wiser now.'

'Mmm, and you're gorgeous. You'll still be gorgeous when we're eighty. You'll still make my knees weak and my heart beat faster. Always.' He stole a kiss. 'I meant it. I love Ty as well. I look at him, and I see you. And I see a bright, quirky little boy who loves all the things I love. And I want to be his father. I mean, I know I can't take the place of Jack, but—'

She pressed a finger to his lips. 'Believe me, simple biology doesn't make someone a father. It's a lot more than that. Ty doesn't even remember Jack. You've done more with Tyler in the past couple of months than his father has done in years. You've helped him with swimming and riding, you've taught him to play chess, you listen to him when he comes home from school, you talk to him about his artwork and horses and knights. And I know he thinks a lot of you because he spends almost as much time talking about you as he does about horses.'

'So, if Ty's happy with the idea, would you consider marrying me?'

She smiled, a teasing light in her eyes. 'Ask me properly, Dr Hurst, and I'll give you your answer.'

'Then I'll talk to him,' Dominic said. 'Man to man.' He smiled. 'In the normal scheme of things, I would be asking your father for your hand in marriage. But, in this case, I think I need to ask your son.'

She stroked his face. 'That's another thing I love about you. You're thoughtful. You consider other people's feelings. Oh, and for the record, my parents think you're wonderful and my mum's already given us their blessing. She guessed a long time ago how I feel about you.'

'Then let's hope,' Dominic said, 'that Ty feels the same.'

The following evening, Dominic was playing chess with Tyler while Louisa was pottering about in the kitchen. His mouth was dry, his skin was prickling, and he could never, ever remember feeling this nervous before. Not when he'd been sitting exams or taking his driving test, because he'd had a fair idea what he was doing and had been able to judge whether he was getting it right. Not when he'd started his first job, because back then he'd known that he still had a lot to learn and it was fine to ask questions as long as you put the patient's needs first.

Right here and now, he felt all at sea.

Because, even though he thought he knew how Tyler would react to his question, he didn't know for certain. And it scared him to death that he might be wrong.

'You're letting me win, aren't you?' Tyler asked, moving his knight. 'Check.'

'I wouldn't insult you like that,' Dominic said. 'But, I admit, I'm not giving the game my full attention.'

'Why not?'

'Because there's something I need to talk to you about. Something serious. Man to man.'

Tyler frowned. 'What?'

This was the biggie. Dominic took a deep breath. 'How would you feel about your mum getting married?'

'Would that mean I'd have a new dad?' Tyler asked carefully.

'Yes. One who'd love you every bit as much as if he'd always been your dad.'

Tyler thought about it. 'Do you mean you?'

Dominic nodded. 'But I'm not going to ask your

mum to marry me unless you're happy about the idea. So I'm asking your permission to propose to your mum.'

'You mean, like a knight used to ask the king?' Tyler said reflectively. 'Except you're a knight and I'm your page. So I'm not really the king.'

'True,' Dominic said, 'but this is your mum we're talking about, so this is a special case. It means I need to ask you first.'

'Are you going to have a baby?'

Dominic coughed. 'No.' But the idea of Louisa's belly all rounded with his child sent a shaft of pure longing through him.

Tyler looked thoughtful. 'I'd like a little brother. Or a sister. And a puppy.'

Dominic laughed. 'I'll see what I can do. Not a wolfhound,' he was quick to add, 'but I think we could talk your mum round on the puppy front.' He paused. 'So was that a yes?'

'My mum smiles a lot more when you're around. And I think I'd like you to be my dad—as long as I can still be your page.' His brow furrowed. 'Because knights used to send their son to be someone else's page, didn't they?'

'Not in this case. You'll be my son *and* my

page,' Dominic promised. 'And, in case you were wondering, I don't approve of the old knightly custom of sending your son to grow up in someone else's castle. You'll be with your mum and me.' He smiled. 'Though my parents live in a castle, so you might get to stay there from time to time. Probably in my old bedroom, in the turret.'

'That's way cool,' Tyler breathed, his eyes wide.

'So do I have your permission to ask your mum to marry me?'

Tyler nodded. 'When are you going to ask her?'

'I was waiting to see how you felt about it first.' He smiled. 'If you've got any ideas about the best time, I'm all ears.'

'Christmas,' Tyler said. 'Because she'll say yes. And I'll have a dad for Christmas—the best present ever.'

Dominic hugged him. 'You,' he said, 'are going to grow up to be my joint-best friend with Ric. As well as a son I'm going to be very, very proud of.'

'And I get to call you Dad instead of Dominic?'

'Absolutely.' His heart felt as if it was full to overflowing.

'Good. Because I love you. Dad.' He tested the word and smiled. 'Dad.'

'I love you, too.' Dominic held him close. 'Son.'

And when he went into the kitchen on the pretext of fetching drinks while Tyler dealt the cards, he saw that Louisa's lashes were wet.

'OK, honey?' he asked, concerned.

She cuddled in to him. 'I was eavesdropping. At the end. And…' Tears choked off the rest of her sentence, but he knew they were happy tears.

'I know,' he said softly. 'Me, too. And I can't wait until Christmas.'

The rest of the week flew by. Dominic was working on Christmas Day, but he'd taken Tyler to help him choose a very special present during the week and had sworn his new son to utter secrecy.

His shift was busy, with the expected patients who'd scratched their eyes on Christmas tree branches while retrieving presents, people who'd cut themselves carving the turkey—and one whose knife had slipped off an avocado and into his hand—and children with bits of toys stuck up their noses. But obviously his joy shone through because his patients ended up relaxing and smiling back at him, losing their misery and stress as he treated them.

And at last it was the end of his shift. He drove over to Gillian and Matt Austin's house, where Louisa and Tyler had spent the day, along with her brother Stewart, his wife, Marie, and their twin daughters.

'Merry Christmas.' Louisa met him at the door and kissed him soundly. 'How was your day?'

'Better now I'm with you.' He lifted her up and spun her round.

'Put the girl down,' Gillian teased. She kissed him warmly on the cheek. 'Happy Christmas, love. And thank you for those beautiful lace bobbins. They're perfect.'

'I'm glad you like them. Though I have to admit, I did have a bit of help choosing them,' he admitted. 'From your wonderful daughter.'

He had a mug of coffee and a turkey salad sandwich with the Austins, wished everyone a merry Christmas, and then put Louisa and Tyler's overnight bags into the back of his car before driving them to Amberhurst.

Fairy-lights were threaded through the trees on the approach to the castle.

'It's magical,' Tyler breathed.

'It certainly is.' Dominic exchanged a smile with Louisa.

Milly met them at the door, surrounded by bouncing dogs, and Tyler was utterly delighted by them. He was even more thrilled when he discovered that his bedroom was indeed going to be in one of the turrets.

'We've left your presents under the tree. But I'm afraid we've been terribly rude and already opened ours,' Milly said. 'Thank you so much for the photograph.'

As they went into the drawing room, Louisa could see the silver photo frame she'd bought for Milly, containing the picture of Dominic, Tyler, herself and Pegasus, in pride of place on the mantelpiece.

Milly sorted out a glass of orange juice for Tyler—one with no bits, on Dominic's advice—and Buck's Fizz for Dominic and Louisa, and made sure they were comfortably seated.

'Dominic, can you do the presents, darling?' she asked.

Tyler was thrilled to discover that Milly and Roderick had bought him a deep velvet cloak like Dominic's, and was almost beside himself with joy when he opened Dominic's present. 'It's a real knight's helmet! Thank you so much.'

Oliver and Mina had bought Tyler some more art supplies; and Louisa adored the cashmere sweater that Milly and Roderick had bought her and the silver bracelet from Oliver and Mina.

Dominic handed over a box to Louisa with a slight smile. She opened it, then kissed him soundly. 'Thanks. My camera was on its last legs.' And the one he'd bought her was state of the art.

'What about the other present?' Tyler asked. 'Aren't you going to give her that now?'

Dominic had intended to ask Louisa to marry him, later, under the stars in the garden. But when he saw the expectant look in Tyler's eyes— reflected on the rest of his family's faces—he realised that right here, right now, would be the perfect place and time.

'That isn't actually a Christmas present,'

Dominic said. 'But, since you mention it...' He dropped onto one knee in front of Louisa, and fished the velvet-covered box out of his pocket to reveal the perfect solitaire he and Tyler had chosen together, in a simple but pretty platinum setting. 'Tyler's given me his blessing to ask you, and now feels the right moment. I love you very, very much and I want to spend the rest of my life with you. I want to make a family with you. So please will you do me the honour of becoming my wife and making Tyler my son?'

She stared at him, a sheen of tears in her eyes, then wrapped her arms round him. 'I love you, too. Yes. Yes.' She kissed him. 'Most definitely, yes.'

EPILOGUE

Six months later

ON A hot, sunny day in June, Louisa walked down the aisle of the church at Amberhurst Castle on her father's arm, with Mina, Bea and Mel as her bridesmaids, Tyler as her pageboy and her twin nieces as her flower girls.

Dominic turned round to watch his bride walking towards him. She could see the joy on his face—a joy that was mirrored through the whole congregation. Dominic's mother and her own were both brushing away a tear, her father and Dominic's were both looking proud, Oliver was looking adoringly at his wife, Ric was looking equally adoringly at his own wife, and her brother Stewart was holding hands with Marie, giving Tyler and the twins encouraging smiles.

Life didn't get more perfect than this. Making her wedding vows to Dominic in the place where his family had exchanged those same vows for hundreds of years, and knowing that they had enough love between them to get through anything.

As they signed the register, the tenor who had sung at Oliver and Mina's wedding sang 'You Raise Me Up'. Dominic's hands tightened on his new wife's. 'You make me more than I am,' he said softly.

'Just as you do me,' she said, smiling at him. 'Always.'

'I love you, Mrs Hurst.' And, not caring that it wasn't quite the traditional place to do so in the wedding ceremony, he kissed her.

MEDICAL™

Large Print

Titles for the next six months...

July

SHEIKH, CHILDREN'S DOCTOR...HUSBAND	Meredith Webber
SIX-WEEK MARRIAGE MIRACLE	Jessica Matthews
RESCUED BY THE DREAMY DOC	Amy Andrews
NAVY OFFICER TO FAMILY MAN	Emily Forbes
ST PIRAN'S: ITALIAN SURGEON, FORBIDDEN BRIDE	Margaret McDonagh
THE BABY WHO STOLE THE DOCTOR'S HEART	Dianne Drake

August

CEDAR BLUFF'S MOST ELIGIBLE BACHELOR	Laura Iding
DOCTOR: DIAMOND IN THE ROUGH	Lucy Clark
BECOMING DR BELLINI'S BRIDE	Joanna Neil
MIDWIFE, MOTHER...ITALIAN'S WIFE	Fiona McArthur
ST PIRAN'S: DAREDEVIL, DOCTOR...DAD!	Anne Fraser
SINGLE DAD'S TRIPLE TROUBLE	Fiona Lowe

September

SUMMER SEASIDE WEDDING	Abigail Gordon
REUNITED: A MIRACLE MARRIAGE	Judy Campbell
THE MAN WITH THE LOCKED AWAY HEART	Melanie Milburne
SOCIALITE...OR NURSE IN A MILLION?	Molly Evans
ST PIRAN'S: THE BROODING HEART SURGEON	Alison Roberts
PLAYBOY DOCTOR TO DOTING DAD	Sue MacKay

MEDICAL™

Large Print

October

TAMING DR TEMPEST	Meredith Webber
THE DOCTOR AND THE DEBUTANTE	Anne Fraser
THE HONOURABLE MAVERICK	Alison Roberts
THE UNSUNG HERO	Alison Roberts
ST PIRAN'S: THE FIREMAN AND NURSE LOVEDAY	Kate Hardy
FROM BROODING BOSS TO ADORING DAD	Dianne Drake

November

HER LITTLE SECRET	Carol Marinelli
THE DOCTOR'S DAMSEL IN DISTRESS	Janice Lynn
THE TAMING OF DR ALEX DRAYCOTT	Joanna Neil
THE MAN BEHIND THE BADGE	Sharon Archer
ST PIRAN'S: TINY MIRACLE TWINS	Maggie Kingsley
MAVERICK IN THE ER	Jessica Matthews

December

FLIRTING WITH THE SOCIETY DOCTOR	Janice Lynn
WHEN ONE NIGHT ISN'T ENOUGH	Wendy S. Marcus
MELTING THE ARGENTINE DOCTOR'S HEART	Meredith Webber
SMALL TOWN MARRIAGE MIRACLE	Jennifer Taylor
ST PIRAN'S: PRINCE ON THE CHILDREN'S WARD	Sarah Morgan
HARRY ST CLAIR: ROGUE OR DOCTOR?	Fiona McArthur

MILLS BOON